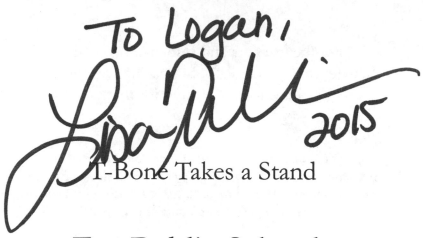

To Logan,

Lisa W. 2015

T-Bone Takes a Stand

For Public Schools

by Lisa Funari-Willever

Franklin Mason Press
Trenton, New Jersey

For the teachers and students who make
New Jersey's public schools amazing and for those
willing to take a stand for them.

*Special thanks to Dawn Hiltner, Anne Salvatore, Wanda
Swanson, Jennifer Wahner, Iris Hutchinson, Allyssa Barnes,
Lauren Lambiase, Marcia Jacobs, Karen Funari, Linda Funari,
and Nancy Byrne...all amazing women.*

Franklin Mason Press ISBN: 978-0-9857218-4-8
Library of Congress Control Number: 2015913387

Text Copyright © 2015 Lisa Funari-Willever

Cover Design by Peri Poloni-Gabriel
www.knockoutbooks.com

Editorial Staff: Shoshana Hurwitz, Iris Hutchinson

TABLE OF CONTENTS

The Nicky Fifth Series

Chapter Books
32 Dandelion Court
Nicky Fifth's Garden State Adventure
Nicky Fifth For Hire
Nicky Fifth's Passport to the Garden State
Nicky Fifth at the Jersey Shore
Nicky Fifth's New Jersey
Nicky Fifth Says Vote For T-Bone
Nicky Fifth Explores New Jersey's Great Outdoors
T-Bone Takes a Stand For Public Schools

Activity Books
Nicky Fifth Explores New Jersey's Great Outdoors
Writing With Lisa Funari-Willever & Friends

Online Activity Books
32 Dandelion Court
Nicky Fifth's Garden State Adventure
Nicky Fifth For Hire
Nicky Fifth's Passport to the Garden State
Nicky Fifth at the Jersey Shore
Nicky Fifth's New Jersey
Nicky Fifth Says Vote For T-Bone
Nicky Fifth Explores New Jersey's Great Outdoors
T-Bone Takes a Stand For Public Schools

A Letter From the Author

Dear readers,

I am so excited to provide you with a book that teaches you about school. It may seem funny to learn about schools when schools are where you do so much of your learning, but maybe that's exactly why we all need to know more about them.

Public schools are more than reading, writing, and math, or gym, art, and recess. They are where kids learn to imagine, create, learn, and explore.

At least that's how it used to be. When I was a student, I remember every project my teachers used from the "Ugly Bug Ball" to our colonial fair. When I was a second and fourth-grade teacher, we turned our lessons into songs and plays. We were encouraged to be creative and use a variety of methods to reach a variety of learners. Sadly, that has been changing.

Today, a rigid curriculum, excessive paperwork, and standardized testing have replaced true learning. It is up to kids and their families to join T-Bone in taking a stand for public schools. As a parent of public school students, I am proud to shed light on the changes that negatively impact children. As an author who visits 60-70 schools each year, I have a unique opportunity to spend time in a wide range of schools each year, and each year I see dedicated teachers, who provide amazing lessons in spite of the changes.

In this book, T-Bone, Nicky, and Wanda will teach readers what really makes all schools, public, private, or charter, succeed. The answers to improving education are not found in a standardized test or yet another new and improved curriculum. The three most important factors have always been parenting, priorities, and poverty. When we decide to work on those issues together, student performance will improve.

Throughout the series, the characters encourage all children to use their voices by getting informed and getting involved. This is an issue that affects everyone, and I hope you will share your thoughts with your families, your school districts, and your lawmakers. We have a great opportunity, if we work together, to resume real learning.

The formula for successful public schools is simple: parents that make education a priority, students that are ready to learn, and a true understanding of how poverty and vastly unequal resources affect students.

New Jersey's public schools have always provided students with a remarkable education, and we must take a stand to protect those public schools.

Warmly,

Lisa Funari-Willever

A portion of each book sale will be donated to the Nicky Fifth Foundation's CODE READ program.

CHAPTER ONE

Four, three, two, one, I counted in my head. I was sure that by the time I reached one, T-Bone would be walking through my front door. I was usually pretty good at predicting the exact moment of his arrival. Call it a knack or a sixth sense, but whatever it was, it must have been off today. I poked my head out the front door. I glanced up and down the street; still no sign of T-Bone. Very, very strange, I thought as I turned around to head toward the kitchen.

"Hey, Nick, what's up?" he asked, standing right in front of me with his usual goofy grin. I shrieked and jumped back, not expecting anyone to be standing there.

"Are you crazy?" I yelled, trying to catch my breath. "You can't just sneak up on a guy in his own house!"

"Crazy?" he asked, tilting his head toward the ceiling. "No, I'm not crazy, and I'm pretty sure you can't sneak up on someone who's expecting you."

"Except," I uttered, "that I was expecting you to come through the front door. I was expecting you to make some noise. How'd you even get in here? Did you slide down the chimney or just break a window?"

"If you must know," he began, "I came in through the back door. I thought I'd change things up. And by the way, you should really see a doctor. You're really breathing heavy!"

"I don't need a doctor," I mumbled, "just a normal friend."

"Normal is totally overrated and, in my opinion, pretty boring," he laughed. "So now that we both know I'm here, I have big news!"

"What's your big news?" I wondered out loud. "The air freshener people got all of your letters and they're finally bringing back mango-coconut-papaya?"

"No, nothing that big," he shrugged. "But I wish they would. Who gets rid of an air freshener that smells like summer, Hawaii, and happiness?"

"So your news?" I repeated.

"Oh yeah, this is exciting! I found a really cool website."

"Oh no," I said. "I really, really hope it's not the *How to Become a Millionaire in Three Days Without Leaving Your House* website again."

"No," he said. "That one might actually be a scam. Believe it or not, not everything on the Internet is true."

"Really? Everything on the Internet isn't true?" I sarcastically asked, shaking my head in disbelief. "I hope it's not that website that guaranteed you could become a successful sheep herder and make millions selling wool?"

"No, it's not that one either," he replied. "And, in my defense, that one could probably work; it's just hard to tell without actually owning sheep or a farm."

"Then I give up," I exclaimed. "What hair-brained, get-rich-quick scheme have you stumbled upon this time?"

"It's called *Crossroads of the Revolution* and they have a great section called *Meet Your Revolutionary Neighbors*."

I immediately paused and looked up. I actually knew all about this website. It did what many kids considered impossible: it made history fun. If you wanted to know about the brave New Jersey citizens who made important contributions to our country, this was the best site.

"They have biographies, and you can even find out which neighbors were patriots who supported the colonists' fight for freedom and which neighbors were loyalists who supported the king of England," T-Bone explained. "They have so many interesting revolutionary New Jersey things on their site."

"I know. It's amazing," I agreed.

"Here, I'll show you," he said as he headed toward our computer. "I just can't remember the web address."

"Revolutionary New Jersey," I said.

"Yeah, we already covered that," he nodded. "New Jersey is revolutionary. Now let me think of the address."

"Revolutionary New Jersey," I repeated.

"Wow, you're like a broken record," he sighed. "Yes, New Jersey is revolutionary. I get it. Now if you're really quiet, I'll be able to think of the website's address. It's on the tip of my tongue."

"T-Bone, the address is **revolutionarynj.org**."

"Oh," he laughed, "that's it! Why didn't you say anything? Yesterday, I was on the website reading about a guy named Joseph Borden. Does that name ring any bells?"

"Sure, he was a patriot. What's now called Bordentown was once named Borden's Towne," I replied. "We should include it in one of our reports so other kids know about it."

"That's a good idea," said T-Bone, "but I have a better idea. I actually have an unbelievable idea. In fact, if I don't say so myself, it's a remarkable idea."

"You're not gonna start juicing all of your food again, are you?" I asked, remembering his attempt to drink a burger.

"No, this is even bigger," he insisted. "Way bigger. I wanna become a Revolutionary Neighbor. I wanna take a stand about something big and important."

"Do you want me to give you the good news first or the bad news first?" I asked.

"Well, I think bad news after good news spoils the good news, but good news after bad news can cheer you up," he replied. "So I'll definitely take the bad news first."

"Okay," I began, "the bad news is that you're a couple of centuries too late to be a Revolutionary Neighbor."

"But I love how brave everyone was during the Revolution," he insisted. "I love how they all got behind a good cause."

"You do realize they didn't *all* get behind the good cause, right?" I corrected him. "The colonies had plenty of loyalists, like William Franklin, who stood by the king."

"You're right," he shrugged, suddenly looking pretty sad.

"But remember, there's the good news," I quickly reminded him. "The Revolutionary War didn't solve every issue our country faced or would face. So that means there's still plenty of issues to take a stand about."

"Like what?" he mumbled. "I'm too late to take a stand against the Quartering Act or the Stamp Act. And if I can't even protest taxation without representation, what's left?"

"Are you serious?" I asked. "There are so many problems in the world that need people with a revolutionary spirit to join their cause. It's simple; you just need to decide what your cause will be, get informed, then get involved."

I felt like Paul Revere and the Sons of Liberty, urging people to join the cause. The only difference was that I didn't even know what cause I was urging him to join. For T-Bone, it was in his blood. He truly wanted to right wrongs and make the world a better place. He was like Robin Hood minus the band of merry men. He just needed to find his cause.

I had known T-Bone since I moved to New Jersey. When it came to helping, he had a one-track mind. The only time he wasn't thinking of how he could improve the world was when he was thinking about Wanda Heiss. From the moment they met, he saw fireworks every time he looked in her direction. My first impression of Wanda was bossy-know-it-all. Not T-Bone; he saw smart and independent. When they ran against each other for student council president, I knew it would be a tight race. I was his campaign manager, and I still have no idea who actually got the most votes. When the principal announced that, for the first time ever, there would be two co-presidents, I was sure it had to be T-Bone's idea. Even though he never admitted that he gave her the co-presidency, I truly believed she would not have done the same for him. I blamed the fruity shampoos her parents bought her. T-Bone turned into a lovesick puppy whenever he smelled her fruit-scented hair.

Before I got used to the idea of co-presidents, T-Bone had invited her to join us as the *Unofficial Junior Ambassadors* of New Jersey. I was fully prepared to veto his idea until my grandfather reminded me that our goal was to make every kid in the state a proud ambassador. What really convinced me to go along with his plan was the simple fact that she did not love T-Bone. As hard as he tried, she just didn't feel the same way. That made me happy. I wasn't happy because his heart was constantly broken, but I was relieved. As long as Wanda didn't fall in love with T-Bone, there would be no major distractions. After all, we still had *At Your Service*, our odd-job business, we had the ambassador jobs, and of course, there was school. Thankfully, they wouldn't be staring at each other and inventing adorable pet names any time soon. Instead, he just followed her around a lot, and she just rolled her eyes a lot.

Luckily, Wanda was really smart and very organized. Since our ambassador job was to find, visit, and report on amazing New Jersey places, and Wanda loved New Jersey, she turned out to be a perfect fit. And of course, since she didn't love T-Bone, that made her even more perfect.

Before we could brainstorm T-Bone's possible causes, my mom emerged from the kitchen. She had the phone cradled between her shoulder and her ear, and she was motioning for us to sit down for dinner. As usual, T-Bone was the first person sitting at the table. Despite my mom's polite attempts to excuse herself from a very determined telemarketer, my dad walked in, grabbed the phone, and hung it up. While there was a long list of things that got on my dad's nerves, and T-Bone was near the top of that list, telemarketers who called during dinner were at the very top.

"Hon, I hate to be rude to them," my mom sighed as she set down a large salad bowl. "They're just doing their jobs."

"And making sure we eat without interruptions is one of my jobs," he said with a firm nod. "So what are we having tonight? It smells great in here."

"It sure does," T-Bone agreed as he sniffed the air.

"Oh, look," said my dad, "Tommy is joining us. Again."

"Wouldn't miss it, Mr. A.," T-Bone said with a big smile.

"Tommy, do your parents ever wonder where you are?" my dad asked. "Don't they miss seeing you at the dinner table every night?"

My mom quickly turned around and gave my dad the *don't-be-rude* look.

"Don't worry about me, Mr. A.," T-Bone reassured him, "my family eats dinner pretty late."

"So, you eat two dinners every night?" my dad shrieked.

"Usually," he said. "Unless I don't like my mom's dinner."

"So then you only eat one meal?" my dad continued.

"Kinda," T-Bone smiled. "I just eat twice as much here."

Before my dad could say anything else, my mom placed a beautiful lasagna on the table. It looked perfect: crisp, but not burnt. Every noodle strip was perfectly in place. As my brother, Timmy, and my sisters, Maggie and Emma, sat down, my dad and I stared at her perfect lasagna. After a moment, we realized it was a little *too* perfect.

"Erin, did you make this lasagna?" asked my dad.

"That's a strange question," she said, without ever answering the question.

"It looks too perfect," I observed. "Did *you* make this?"

"Define make," she said still avoiding the real question.

"Hmmm," my dad said as he examined the masterpiece in front of us. "If I didn't know any better, I would guess that you're now defining *making* as *heating up*."

"Can't cook a lasagna without heat, now can we?" she answered with a shrug. "Now let's eat before it gets cold!"

"Wait a minute," Timmy wondered out loud as he examined the kitchen. "Where's the big mess? The kitchen's too clean."

"Okay, okay," she confessed, "I picked it up after school. It was this or hot dogs. But don't worry, I had a coupon."

"Well, it smells delicious," said my dad, aware that his teasing might upset her. "Oh, and good job using the coupon."

Since September, our meals were becoming more casual. For years, my mom taught kindergarten, and she really loved teaching the little kids. Last year, however, she was moved to fourth grade and, ever since, things had changed. She got in later and later each day, she was baking less, and sometimes we heard the vacuum cleaner at midnight. One day, when I came home from school, I found a box of cereal in the refrigerator and a gallon of milk on the pantry shelf. We weren't sure if it was the stress of being in a new grade or if there was more going on. Never complaining, she just kept smiling and telling us that it was all coming together.

As my dad tried to ask about her day, T-Bone cut him off.

"Mrs. A., I've been trying to find something to take a stand for, and thanks to you, I now have it," he announced.

"A stand?" my mom asked.

"You know, a cause," he explained. "Like our Revolutionary Neighbors did a couple of years ago."

"You mean a couple of centuries ago," Timmy corrected.

"Either way," T-Bone continued, "I'm gonna take a stand to make restaurant food look less perfect so families will believe its homemade. This is so awesome!"

The room went silent. Of all the issues that T-Bone could choose, he chose overly neat restaurant take-out food.

"Tommy, what are you talking about?" asked my dad. "You can't take a stand against attractive food."

"Okay," he said, quickly trying to think of a new plan. "I've got it. I'll take a stand against newspaper comic strips."

"What?" asked my dad. "Did you say comic strips?"

"Sure," said T-Bone. "Why do they only have color comics on Sundays? This is an issue everyone will get behind."

"Yay, color comics every day," Maggie cheered. "Finally!"

"Yay, what Maggie said," Emma chimed in.

"Okay, now I'll ask you, Nick," my dad said as he slowly turned in my direction. "What is he talking about?"

"He wants to take a stand about something important and make it his cause," I explained.

"Tommy," my mom said in her gentler, more kindergartenish tone, "I don't think black and white comics are really an important issue. Maybe you need to keep thinking about this. Maybe you should sleep on the problem."

"Take a stand against bad mattresses?" he said, jumping out of his seat. "Why didn't I think of that? It's brilliant!"

"No," she smiled. "Give this whole taking a stand idea more time. I'm sure you'll think of something great."

While dinner was delicious, it was the quietest we had ever seen T-Bone. Even though no one was complaining, I knew why he was so quiet. He was desperately trying to think of a cause that was actually important to a lot of people. When dinner was over, we all helped my mom clean up. As soon as we finished, T-Bone thanked my parents and ran out the front door.

"Why is he running?" asked my dad.

"I don't know," I said with a shrug. "He proably doesn't want to be late for dinner."

CHAPTER TWO

On the bus the next morning, T-Bone was still quiet. There was no way he could still be thinking of an issue, I thought, trying to remember the other times he was this quiet. There was the time they discontinued the *mango-coconut-papaya* air freshener. There was the time his brothers used his favorite suit to dress a scarecrow. Then there was the time he realized he was too young to run for the Senate. I wasn't sure if I should leave him alone or cheer him up. I decided I should at least try to cheer him up.

"Hey, how was your second dinner?" I asked.

"I'm sure it was good," he mumbled, looking straight ahead.

"What happened?" I wondered. "Get there too late?"

"No," he sighed. "I was on time, and I ate it. I just don't remember thinking about it when I ate it."

Unfortunately, as the day went on, T-Bone's mood did not improve. By lunch, I decided to take matters into my own hands. Desperate times called for desperate measures. We had reached Defcon 5, so I snuck off and made my move.

"Wanda, do you have a second?" I motioned from behind the vending machines.

"What are you doing back there?" she whispered, slowly peeking around the corner.

Wanda and I had seen this before. T-Bone would get so excited about some kind of good deed and then get crushed when he hit a roadblock. We even developed the T-Bone Color Code System. Yellow meant he seemed disappointed. It was like when you reach into a bag of chips only to find someone put an empty bag back on the shelf. Disappointing, but not the end of the world. Yellow was very common, and we ignored it. Orange meant he was a little down, like when he realized he hadn't done anything worthy of a nomination to the New Jersey Hall of Fame. Red, however, was major. It happened whenever a letter came from Billy in the governor's office. T-Bone always saw it and assumed that it was good news about the bill to name us Official Junior Ambassadors. Sadly, it was always something else.

"We have a code," I whispered.

"Oh no," she sighed. "How bad?"

"Flaming red!" I said. "Fire-truck, candy-apple RED!"

"What?" she gasped. "Our scale doesn't even go that high!"

"I know," I nodded. "Can you come over after school? Maybe planning our next day trip will cheer him up."

"Sure," she said. "I always have my New Jersey binder in my bag, so I can come right from the bus."

"You always carry that with you?" I asked, realizing it was a dumb question as soon as I said it. This was Wanda; of course she carried the binder everywhere.

Since she had a habit of not answering dumb questions, she just shook her head, rolled her eyes and then walked away. I waited a few minutes to make sure T-Bone didn't see me talking to her without him. If he saw us talking, he would think I loved her, and that would be bad. We'd definitely need a new code for that one, like surface of the sun.

When I returned to our table, T-Bone was just sitting there, staring straight ahead. He hadn't even touched his lunch. When I told him we should all get together to discuss our next day trip, he simply nodded. I decided to give him some time to come around. Worst case, I'd just have to wait until he saw Wanda at my house. That always did the trick.

By the end of the day, T-Bone was still hovering around the flaming-red level. He said he needed to stop home before coming over. It was usually to dip himself in his dad's aftershave to impress Wanda. While the smell was both awful and overwhelming, it would be a good sign that he was snapping out of a bad mood.

I was only home for five minutes when the doorbell rang. Surprisingly, it was Wanda. I couldn't believe she beat T-Bone. That was a first.

"Hi, Nick," she said as she began unpacking her bag.

"Listen, before T-Bone gets here," I whispered, "he's really down in the dumps. It's pretty bad."

"Why is he so down?" she asked as she sharpened a dozen pencils. "Is it the air freshener thing again?"

"No, it's worse. He was so inspired by the *Crossroads of the Revolution* website and the Revolutionary Neighbors that he wanted to become a Revolutionary Neighbor himself."

"Perfect," she rolled her eyes. "He's only a couple hundred years too late."

"Yeah, I know," I laughed. "We went over that. So now he wants to take a stand about an important issue like they did."

"And let me guess," she wondered out loud, "he can't think of a non-ridiculous issue? Am I getting warmer?"

"We have a winner!" I replied. "We need to help him come up with an issue and quick."

"That shouldn't be hard," she said while shaking her head. "Worthy issues are kind of everywhere."

A moment later, the doorbell rang. Wanda assumed it was T-Bone, but I figured it was a delivery. T-Bone never rang a doorbell, knocked, or even paused before coming in.

"I'm coming," I yelled.

Surprisingly, it wasn't the mailman. It was T-Bone.

"May I come in?" he asked.

"Why'd you ring the bell, and why are you asking if you can come in?" I wondered, totally confused.

"I don't know," he said. "That's what ordinary people do."

I noticed that he didn't smell like his dad's aftershave. While my nose, my eyes, and our houseplants were grateful, I knew it was a bad sign. Wanda immediately started talking to him.

"Hi, T-Bone," she said as she organized a stack of papers. "What's up?"

"Nothing," he sighed as he plopped onto the couch. "I'm just an ordinary guy having an ordinary day. That's all."

Wanda looked as puzzled as I did. This was new territory. I decided to stick with the plan and began discussing our next day trip. I suggested Bordentown since he was excited about our Revolutionary Neighbor Joseph Borden.

"I've been to some street festivals in Bordentown," said Wanda. "The main street is called Farnsworth Avenue, and the town is filled with history."

"We went there before," I remembered. "We even went to an ice cream place that was inside an old bank. I really liked that town. What do you think, Mr. Ordinary?"

"Sure," he mumbled without even looking at us.

"If I remember correctly, there's a statue of Thomas Paine," I added. "Remember him? He wrote *Common Sense*."

"He wasn't ordinary," said T-Bone. "He was extraordinary."

"All right, spill it," Wanda demanded. "What's wrong?"

"Nothing," he replied.

Treating him like my stubborn little sisters, I offered him a popsicle. I thought it was best to be subtle.

"Okay," she began, "this is ridiculous. Nicky told me this is all because you wanted to be some kind of Revolutionary Neighbor. Is that about right?"

Way to be subtle, I thought.

"Yeah," he shrugged, "but, I was born too late. I would have been a great colonist. There were fewer people in the country; I could have been a standout, an all-star. Now I'm just a nobody, born too late to do anything important."

Wanda started to laugh.

"What's so funny?" he asked.

I was hoping she had a good answer.

"*You're* funny," she said as she shook her head. "*You're* hysterical. Are you really going to tell me that you could only change the world if you were born in the 1700s?"

"Yeah," he shook his head. "I think that's what I'm saying. Wait, yes, that's what I'm saying. I think."

Wanda was like a TV detective. She wasn't just a great lie detector, she was good at making you question yourself, even when you were sure about something.

"Okay, T-Bone," she declared, "pay attention because I'm not going to repeat this. Our Founding Fathers started this country, but it takes people from every generation to keep it going. If all of the talented people lived in the 1700s, what would have happened to this country in the 1800s or the 1900s? And it's not just America. The world has so many problems right now, and we need smart, dedicated people to solve those problems. Are you going to sulk and give up because you were just too lazy to find a great cause?"

Harsh, I thought. I was afraid to look at T-Bone because I thought he might be crying. I was pretty sure I would have been. When she swung around and stood six inches from his nose, I thought he would faint.

"The only reason I agreed to be your co-president and ambassador assistant," she continued, "was because I think you have an amazing heart, great ideas, and you never give up. At least until now, that is. Are you giving up now, T-Bone? Are you going to be like the millions of people who just go about their business and give little thought to the world around them? Are you going to sit back and assume everyone else will do the heavy lifting? What's it going to be, T-Bone? Do you want to be part of the solution? Because if you're not, then you're part of the problem."

I could picture Wanda in a locker room giving a halftime speech. Before he could answer, my mom walked in from the kitchen, holding stacks of folders. She gently set them down, blew the hair out of her eyes, and looked at T-Bone.

"Tommy, did I overhear correctly," she asked. "Are you really giving up because you can't find an issue? Because if you need an issue, I'll give you an issue. How about public schools? You attend public schools. Notice any changes? Have you noticed anything that needs attention? Anything?"

He was getting bombarded. I was glad I wasn't him. There was no way I wanted Wanda and my mom glaring at me like that. I couldn't believe he wasn't crying. Poor guy, I thought.

"Well, I was...I mean, I thought," T-Bone stammered. My usually articulate friend who has no problem speaking was tongue-tied. That's when their attention turned to me.

"And honestly, Nick," my mom looked at me, "you don't see public education as an area that could use your voices?"

"Well, I was, I mean, I thought. Huh?" I asked.

Before she could answer me, my mom returned to the kitchen to start making dinner. What just happened? T-Bone looked as confused as I was, but then he spoke.

"Your mom is right," he said quietly.

"What?" I asked, still in shock.

"Your mom is one hundred percent right. Wanda is too," he replied. "Public schools are the foundation of society. Nothing affects our country more than education."

"And nothing hurts our country more than hurting public schools," Wanda chimed in as she shuffled her papers.

In an instant, T-Bone was sitting at the kitchen table, asking my mom about her thoughts on public schools.

"Tommy," she began, "today's public schools are where we prepare children to become productive, contributing, and independent members of society and a global community."

"Exactly," he said. "It's all about reading, writing, and math."

"No," she continued, "it's more than reading, writing, and math. Schools should be where students learn to think, to question, and to imagine. Without creativity, there can never be innovation. Teachers desperately want to encourage creativity and problem solving."

"So it's not about reading, writing, and math?" he asked.

My mom stopped all of her dinner preparation and stood still. Lately, she had been so frustrated with ideas and laws that affected her students. I could sense her frustration was about to spill over. As I pulled up a chair, Wanda grabbed a notebook and started taking notes. Most prepared girl in the world, I thought.

"Okay, think about education this way," she said. "Children absolutely need to know the basics. Reading, writing, and math are the keys to functioning in life, but what happens in a classroom allows people to use that knowledge to solve problems. Lawmakers and businesses tend to forget that teaching is an art, it's not a science."

"Oh, I get it," T-Bone nodded. "You're really upset because you believe schools should skip science and focus on art?"

"No," she replied. "When I say teaching is not a science, it's because it's very hard to repeat anything in a classroom like you would in a science experiment. It's different because a class is a living thing made up of lots of living things."

"Like plants, bugs, and germs?" he interrupted. "That's why I always use hand sanitizer."

"No, like students," she continued. "And every day, students arrive in different moods, with different issues, different abilities, and different interests. When you have over twenty students in front of you, things not only change year to year and day to day, but often hour to hour."

"Huh?" asked T-Bone. "Why do the same kids change?"

"Because they're people," Wanda interrupted. "Mrs. A., do you mean that one day two kids don't feel well, three kids are tired, and one is confused? Then the next day, three different kids are confused, two different kids don't feel well, and two different kids are tired?"

"Exactly," my mom sighed. "Teaching is an art because students are living, breathing people who are constantly changing. The art of teaching is being able to teach a lesson while constantly adapting to changing moods, abilities, and needs. It's that ability to adapt that makes teachers so necessary. That's why they can never be replaced by computers, robots, and no, Tommy, not even the most awesome holograms."

"Holograms would be cool," T-Bone foolishly commented. "Nick, can you imagine a hologram teacher?"

I decided it was in my best interest to ignore him.

"T-Bone, teaching is one of the most difficult and one of the most important jobs on the planet," said Wanda.

"It's not oil rigs, tuna fishing, and firefighting?" he asked.

"Those are the most dangerous jobs," I whispered, hoping he would just stop talking. No such luck.

"Hmm," he thought out loud, "I thought they gave you a teacher's guide, and you get all of the answers. I always thought teaching was really easy since, you know, you have the big desk and all of the answers."

"Having the answers doesn't make someone a good teacher," my mom replied. "And neither does a big desk."

"Don't those huge teacher's guides tell you exactly what to do?" he asked. "It sounds pretty predictable?"

"Well, if I was working on an assembly line and building cars," she explained, "I would be able to repeat the same activity all day long, every day, and it would work out as planned. That would make teaching more like a science, or something that can be repeated."

"Hey, wait," said T-Bone, "teachers have lesson plans. So if you write it down and follow it, then isn't it like science?"

"I think you're looking at lesson plans all wrong," my mom smiled, completely understanding the confusion. "We used to write lesson plans so we knew what we were teaching, how we would teach the lessons, and what materials we would use. Then someone thought we should add every skill we covered. Eventually, writing lesson plans became more like writing a long script."

"Is that bad?" I asked. "Actors use scripts."

"It's about letting teachers teach," she laughed. "All of the added paperwork takes away from the creativity of planning lessons. Some lawmakers have forgotten that teachers are college-educated professionals trained in the art of teaching. The laws they create to improve education are often the exact thing that hurts learning and really hurts students."

"Mrs. A., you are awesome!" T-Bone exclaimed as he jumped out of his seat. "You did it! You really did it! You gave me an issue. I can't believe I was so worried, but now I have my cause. I'm going to take a stand for public schools!"

"Well, Tommy, I'm happy I could help you," she smiled. "I apologize if I sounded frustrated. It's only because I happen to be really frustrated."

"That's okay," T-Bone gushed. "And look at the bright side:

with this new cause, I'll be here all the time, asking you questions, picking your brain, discussing ideas. Isn't it great?"

Suddenly, my mom realized what she had just done. "Yes, Tommy, this is just great, really great."

Somehow, I doubted my father would agree.

CHAPTER THREE

Luckily, for my mom, T-Bone couldn't stay for dinner and raced out of the house after our discussion. Wanda stayed behind to pack up her things and offered a great suggestion for an upcoming day trip. She thought we should explore a town that made a significant impact on public schools in New Jersey. I thought it was a great idea. Knowing Wanda, I knew she'd have something prepared by lunch the next day.

I was relieved that T-Bone was happy again. When he had a good idea, he was like a force of nature, like a tornado or a hurricane. He was Hurricane T-Bone. It was kind of fun to watch. I didn't know exactly how this would turn out, but I was sure kids would be talking about public schools with each other and their parents by the time he was done.

That night, my grandparents stopped by. The first thing Pop asked was where T-Bone was hiding. I told him about Code Flaming Red and T-Bone's cause. He was the only one, besides me and Wanda, that knew about the T-Bone codes.

"Hmm," he started, "public schools are a great issue. I'm glad to see you kids are taking a stand."

"Well, it started out as T-Bone taking a stand for public schools, but Wanda and I are on board," I explained.

"Luckily, you have a great teacher to tell you what makes public schools work," he said, winking at my mom.

"I am a great teacher," Maggie yelled as she jumped off of the couch. "Watch this."

Maggie grabbed Emma and stood her in the middle of the living room. She looked like a crazy magician ready to make her assistant disappear. Emma stood there, unsure of what would happen next. She had one sock on, and her pigtails looked like an antenna after a storm. The left pigtail had shifted to the top of her head while the right pigtail was below her ear. Since Maggie made Emma play school with her every day, we were waiting for the alphabet song or a counting demonstration.

"My name is Mrs. Abruzzi," Maggie announced. "And this is one of my students; her name is Suzy."

"My name is *not not* Suzy," Emma protested. "My name is Emma."

"No, it's not," Maggie insisted. "I changed it. Your name is Suzy. Suzy Coozy."

"I am *not not* Suzy Coozy," Emma yelled. "I Emma Bruzi!"

We always laughed when Emma tried to say her name. It sounded like she was saying M. Abruzzi. For some reason, Maggie enjoyed changing her name every day. This week she had been Lucy Coozy, Snoozy Coozy, and Newsy Coozy.

"We've been very busy learning lots of stuff in my school," Maggie continued, ignoring Emma's protests. "Now I'll show you what I teached Suzy. Okay, Suzy, roll over."

Before we knew it, Emma was rolling over like a poodle. I thought it was kind of funny; she didn't like her name being changed, but she had no problem rolling around like a circus dog. Kids, I thought.

"Give me your paw," Maggie instructed.

And with that, Emma put out her hand. At that moment, my dad walked into the room. He was just in time to see Emma begging for a pretend dog biscuit.

"Let me guess," he laughed. "Mrs. Abruzzi is teaching Gluesy Croozy?"

"More like training," my mom giggled. "And it's Suzy Coozy today."

After the dog show, I sat out front with Pop. I wondered how much school had changed since he was my age. When

I asked him, he rubbed his forehead and said it was hard to believe how much everything had changed over the years.

"You know, Nicky," he began, "when I was in school, the world was a different place. The skills we needed were different, jobs were different, and technology was different. Heck, our television picture was in black and white."

"So everything really has changed?" I asked.

"No, not everything," he said, sipping his lemonade. "The most important thing in education hasn't changed."

"What's the most important thing?" I asked.

"Children are," he replied, "and they haven't changed. That's a fact that I wish the people in charge would remember."

"What do you mean?" I asked.

"Well, Nick, children have always been filled with wonder and curiosity. Those first five years, before kids even start kindergarten, are so important. Their brains are developing so quickly, quicker than any other time in life. They need to be spoken to every day. They need to be read to every day. They even need to be sung to every day. They may not be talking back, but they sure are listening and learning."

"Has that changed?" I asked, remembering how my mom always sang to us and read us stories.

"Sadly, for many kids it has," he said. "So many kids start school unprepared for learning. When they find themselves in a class where other kids are well prepared, they're at a disadvantage. It's very easy to fall behind but very, very difficult to catch up."

"Why are so many kids unprepared for kindergarten?" I wondered. "Doesn't *Sesame Street* cover everything?"

I remembered how much I loved watching that show. I had every DVD and knew every line. My mom was convinced that Big Bird taught me the alphabet and the Count taught me to count. That was probably true because whenever I finished counting I said, *"Ah-ha-ha."*

"I agree with you about *Sesame Street*," he said, "it's a great tool to help teach little kids."

"Then why are they so unprepared?"

"Oh, lots of reasons," he continued. "Poverty is a very big reason that people tend to ignore. Some children are born into extreme poverty, and their parents don't have the resources to prepare them. Often, their parents were born without the resources needed to prepare them. You need to understand that for many, poverty is multigenerational. Do you know what that means?"

"I'm not one hundred percent sure," I admitted, even though I wasn't even one percent sure.

"It means it's passed down from one generation to another. Children who are born into extreme poverty don't have the resources or advantages that other kids have. Their children are then born into poverty, and the cycle continues. Did you know some studies show that children in suburban homes often have seventeen age-appropriate books, for each child in the home. But in inner cities, where you have high poverty, it's often one book per three hundred children."

"Holy moly," I said, thinking about the bookcase in my room that was overstuffed with books. Then I thought about the bookcases in my brother and sisters' rooms. Having a teacher for a mother, we must have had hundreds of books. "You mean some kids really don't have *any* books at home?"

"Unfortunately, that's exactly what I mean. It puts so many children at a disadvantage, but books aren't the only thing. Some children don't even have enough food to eat."

"Do you mean like the kids in other countries?" I asked, remembering a commercial I saw on television.

"Yes, and right here in the United States," he said. "There are kids in New Jersey who have breakfast and lunch at school and don't eat again until the next morning. Our old neighbor was an inner-city teacher for years, and she would tell us some of the most heartbreaking stories about her students. I remember she told us about a little boy named Johnny who lived in a room that his mom rented. Johnny, his mom, and his little brother lived in this tiny room, and they didn't have enough food money to last the whole month. Our neighbor would bring food from home and sneak it in his backpack at the end of the day."

"Are you serious?" I asked, suddenly feeling guilty because I had so many books and a kitchen full of food. "That's terrible. How can kids learn when they're hungry? I can't even think when I'm hungry."

"Kiddo, that's just the tip of the iceberg. Many of her students went to a dozen schools by the time they reached the fifth grade, often in the same district. If their families couldn't pay their rent, they would be evicted and move somewhere else, often with friends or family members. They moved around so much, just trying to survive."

"It must be so hard to keep switching schools," I agreed. "I was devastated when I moved from Philadelphia to New Jersey, and that was the only time I ever moved."

"There are also kids in the foster care system and homeless kids, too," he explained. "They all deserve an education and the resources to break out of poverty."

"So poverty is the only thing that affects education?" I asked.

"No, no," he shook his head. "In my opinion, and remember I'm just one old man, the three biggest things that affect education are poverty, parenting, and priorities. That means that even kids who don't live in poverty can be affected by parenting. Even though their parents have resources like books and food and a house, if their parents aren't making sure the kids are going to bed at a decent time, eating healthy, doing their homework, and following rules, then those kids are also at a disadvantage. And many families have so many gadgets and gizmos that the families spend very little time talking. Everyone has some kind of device, and some kids use them for hours and hours each day. It's ironic, though, with all of the high-tech ways to communicate, people talk less now than ever."

"What about the priority thing?" I wondered. "Does it mean education has to be a priority?"

"Absolutely," he nodded. "Whether a family is rich or poor, education has to be a priority for a child to succeed. In so many families that are not poor, parents often focus on extracurricular activities. Kids play multiple sports year round, and parents are always split up, driving kids from practice to practice and game to game. They eat dinner in the car and do homework on the run."

"Oh, I get it," I laughed. "My mom told us about a note she got from a parent. He wanted to know how his son would get a soccer scholarship if she kept giving him homework."

"Exactly," my grandfather laughed. "Parents who neglect their kids are a problem, but parents who don't make education a priority are also a problem. Nowadays, everyone is looking for a sports scholarship, not realizing how rare they are, and forgetting all about academic scholarships. It's all about priorities, Nick."

"So what's the solution?" I asked.

"Well, I think we have to stop looking for an easy solution. The truth is, there isn't one solution. The problem, as I see it, is that we have a conflict. It's the art of teaching vs. the business and politics of education. As long as businesses can make money selling things to schools and lawmakers can get votes for promising changes, the students will lose."

"Do you mean the companies that sell paper and pencils?" I guessed.

"No, not supplies," he answered. "I'm talking about programs, massive programs that promise to change everything and even guarantee success."

"Wow, they have programs that guarantee success?" I asked. "Do they really work?"

"No," Pop laughed, "they cost a lot of money, and they turn things upside down, create a lot of paperwork for teachers, and view kids as interchangeable parts on an assembly line. But do they work? Not usually."

"Hey, my mom was talking about an assembly line," I remembered. "She said teaching kids is an art; it's not like working on an assembly line. Each day, the kids are different, and teachers have to adapt. She said it's not like a science experiment that can be repeated over and over with the same result because kids are people, not parts of a machine."

"She's right," he agreed. "Trying to fix problems with new curriculums and more standardized tests is as effective as fixing your broken dishwasher with a shiny new toaster."

"Huh?" I said.

"Well, nowadays, everyone thinks they have the answers to fix schools," he explained. "And most of the ideas involve more tests. The truth is, tests are just one tool in the toolbag to measure how well kids are doing. But they can't fix what's broken. They're as effective as fixing your broken dishwasher with a new toaster. It might be a nice toaster, but it won't fix the dishwasher and wash the dishes. You need the right solution for the right problem."

"Poverty, parenting, and priorities?" I recalled all three.

"Exactly," he said as he patted my head and walked inside.

My grandfather was one of the best people to have real conversations with because he was very good at explaining difficult things. I couldn't wait to tell T-Bone and Wanda everything I learned during our discussion. Then I started to panic. Without Wanda taking notes, I hoped I would remember everything he said. To be on the safe side, I ran upstairs and started writing it all down.

The next morning, T-Bone was back to his old self. In fact, he was talking so fast, he gave himself a terrible case of hiccups. By the time lunch rolled around, he had interviewed all of his teachers. Sadly, he was still hiccupping. Many of his teachers were also parents, so they had opinions on elementary and high school as well as middle school. When Wanda stopped by, she announced that she had interviewed her teachers, too.

"T-Bone, this stand you're taking for public schools is brilliant," she said. Her smile was so big that I worried she might be falling in love with him. "I really do admire your commitment to doing the right thing."

Oh no, I thought. This could be the start of some mushy, romantic relationship. Now she's admiring him? What's next? One milkshake, two straws? Matching sweaters?

"Want to sit down and compare notes?" he winked as he tapped the open seat next to him.

"Nope, I'm good," she said. "But we definitely need to discuss our trip to Bordentown. I went online and found some really interesting information. I think Bordentown City has something for everyone. Docs today work for both of you?"

As usual, we agreed to meet after school. Somehow, my house had become our headquarters, so we never had to ask where we were meeting.

When I finally sat down, I opened my lunch and took a deep breath. All was right with the world. T-Bone was back to his old self, Wanda clearly didn't love him, and we were about to plan another Garden State adventure. Nothing could have ruined that moment, nothing at all.

Except the bell.

CHAPTER FOUR

When we got off the bus, T-Bone told me he'd be over in a few minutes. When he returned, I could smell his dad's aftershave from across the room. Wanda looked at me and shook her head.

"So, Bordentown," T-Bone began, "the Towne of ol' Joseph Borden. What are we thinking?"

"Well," Wanda answered excitedly, "are you familiar with Clara Barton and her schoolhouse?"

"Sure," I nodded.

"Did you also know that schoolhouse was the first free public school in New Jersey?" she continued.

"I thought all public schools were free," said T-Bone. "Didn't Thomas Jefferson include public schools in the Declaration of Independence?"

"No, the Declaration of Independence told England we were declaring our freedom," I laughed. "I think you're thinking of the Constitution, the law of the land."

"Oh yeah, that's what I meant," T-Bone corrected himself. "So public schools are in the Constitution, right? They're probably near the nutrition food pyramid."

"Actually, I was on the National Constitution Center's website," said Wanda. "I read that the Constitution doesn't mention education, and the Supreme Court decided that education is not a fundamental right under it."

"How can education not be a fundamental right?" wondered T-Bone. "What about the nutrition food pyramid?"

"The Founding Fathers felt education was best left to the states," she explained. "It was considered a duty of families. And, no, the food pyramid is not in the Constitution."

"Hold on!" T-Bone exclaimed as he jumped up to make his point. Unfortunately, his feet must have fallen asleep, and he dropped to the ground like a bag of dirt. When Wanda and I turned in his direction, we didn't see him anywhere.

"T-Bone, are you all right?" she asked as she rushed over to help him. "What happened?"

At first, he looked embarrassed and couldn't get up fast enough. When he smelled her shampoo, however, he suddenly grew very weak. I didn't know if he was really hurt until he winked at me. I realized the fall was real, but the moaning and groaning was definitely a little exaggerated.

"Yeah, what happened, T-Bone?" I asked as Wanda uprighted him and ran to get him some water.

"My feet fell asleep," he whispered with a grin. "Wasn't that awesome? Her hair smells amazing."

"What were you about to say before, you know, your unfortunate fall?" I asked.

"Oh, yeah," he remembered, resuming his yelling. "Hold on! What if one kid's family is rich and one kid's family is poor? Won't the rich kid get a better education than the poor kid? Shouldn't every kid get a great education?"

When Wanda re-emerged with a glass of water, T-Bone suddenly looked a little woozy again. This guy should get an Academy Award for Best Actor, I thought. As Wanda tended to his wooziness, she also answered his question. This girl was definitely good at multitasking.

"Education doesn't fall under the federal Constitution, but states include education in their constitutions," she said.

"Does New Jersey include education?" T-Bone asked in a low whimper.

"Absolutely," she said. "If you visit **nj.gov/education**, you can read all about our state's education history. Education has really come a long way; things were much different three hundred years ago."

"You mean they didn't have computers and smart boards, right?" asked T-Bone.

"Computers? Smart boards?" Wanda laughed. "They didn't even have girls in most schools! Back then, only the privileged went to school, and elementary-level teachers only taught reading, writing, and math. Only a few students from rich families could go on to high school."

"Schools with no girls?" asked T-Bone. "That seems kind of unfair."

"Kind of unfair?" asked Wanda in her most sarcastic voice ever. "It wasn't until 1875 that the New Jersey Constitution required the legislature to provide a system of free public schools for all children in the state between the ages of five and eighteen years."

"Phew," T-Bone sighed, horrified at the thought of a school with no Wanda.

As we continued to research Bordentown and education, we learned more about Clara Barton. Most people knew her as the founder of the Red Cross, but with the support of the local Bordentown community, she opened the first free public school in New Jersey. There weren't many students at first, but by the end of the year, the school had almost two hundred students. It was such a success, the community built a new school and hired a man to run it. They actually paid him double Clara's salary.

"What a frustrating story!" said Wanda, as if steam would shoot out of her ears like a cartoon character. "Boy, that burns me up."

"You mean that it took a year for the school to catch on?" asked T-Bone. "They probably needed better commercials."

"No, T-Bone," she glared at him. "That Clara Barton went to all of the trouble to start a school, and as soon as it was successful, she was replaced by a man, and they paid him twice the salary. Do you think that's fair, T-Bone?"

T-Bone just stared at her and shook his head no. He must have been wondering what happened to the sweet girl who tended to his wooziness. In my opinion, he should have known better. Wanda truly believed in equal rights for everyone, and excluding girls was at the top of her list of no-no's. In fact, she considered it *a big no-no.*

"I'm curious," I said, desperately trying to change the subject. "How does a person just go out and start a school?"

"If you visit **Bordetownhistory.org**, you can learn exactly how she did it," Wanda suggested. "It says she visited a friend in Bordentown, and she noticed idle boys all over out on the streets. So she looked for and found the chairman of the school committee."

"But if there was a law that made them provide free public schools for kids from five to eighteen years old," said T-Bone, "why were these idle kids out all over the streets?"

"Funny thing," she explained, "even though the laws for free public schools existed, no one started any schools. They decided to give Clara a ramshackle, one-room schoolhouse and on the first day of school, six children showed up."

"Wow," said T-Bone. "I wonder if she was disappointed. That's not too many students considering the streets were filled with boys who had nothing to do. She should have advertised free ice cream in her commercials."

"First of all," I interjected, "there were no telephones, no television, no e-mails, and no commercials. I'm sure it took a really long time to spread the word."

"And as far as being disappointed, she was probably too busy to notice," Wanda explained. "They spent the first few weeks cleaning up the schoolhouse and getting it ready. In 1852, she had those six children and very little else. Within a few months, she had over two hundred students, with another four hundred on a waiting list. By 1853, there were over six hundred children in the program, receiving lessons from teachers housed in locations all over the city."

"Hey, I did a report about Clara Barton," my brother, Timmy, said as he bounced into the room. "I used this awesome book called *Who Was Clara Barton?* I'll go get it."

When Timmy returned, he had a stack of *Who Was?*, *Where Was?*, and *What Was?* books. The stack was as long as his arm. I immediately thought about the kids in inner cities that didn't even have one book. He placed the stack on the table and began sorting through them. Lately, every time I saw him, he had a book up to his face. I never paid attention to what he was reading, but now I knew.

"Here it is!" he announced as he proudly held up the book. "I read all about her. She was amazing. Except something happened that wasn't very nice."

"What?" said T-Bone. "Did they knock down the one-room schoolhouse?"

"No," Timmy answered. "Her school was such a success that they built a two-story building for six hundred students."

"The new school still sounds nice," said T-Bone.

"It was definitely nice...for the students," Timmy explained with authority. "It wasn't so nice for Clara."

"Why?" I wondered. "I would have thought she'd have been thrilled to have a big building. Oh wait, is this where they...."

My voice trailed off because I realized what was about to happen next, and I didn't want to say it in front of Wanda.

"When she first opened the school," Timmy continued, "she offered to work for free. The townspeople were so happy that, after a few months, the board hired Clara's friend, too and offered to pay them each $250/year. But when they opened the new school, they called it School One and told her the job was too important and too hard for a woman. They hired a man and paid him $600, offering Clara $250 to be his assistant."

We all looked at Wanda, afraid of her reaction.

"Assistant?" she shrieked. "Too hard and too important for a woman? Really? She started the school and made it a success. I think that's hard and important, don't you?"

"Yes," we all said at the same time. "Definitely hard and important."

"Hey, you guys should go to Bordentown," Timmy suggested. "I could go too if you want."

"That's actually what we're planning right now," said Wanda as she regained her composure. "And you should definitely come with us, Timmy. Right, Nick?"

"Abso-definitely," I blurted out, way too afraid to disagree with her.

I wanted to visit the original, one-room schoolhouse, and I wanted to learn more about Thomas Paine and other famous Bordentown residents. It turned out there were many important people who once lived in what is now called Bordentown City.

"Listen to this," Wanda said as she held up the paper in her hand. "Originally called Farnsworth Landing, it was a place for trading along the river. It started with a log cabin on the riverbank and a guy named Thomas Farnsworth in 1682."

"What are the odds of a guy named Thomas Farnsworth living in a place with the same exact name?" asked T-Bone. "It's gotta be a million to one, maybe even a billion to one."

"The town was named *after* him!" I shook my head.

"Or maybe he was named after the town," he suggested. "Sounds like the old chicken and egg dilemma. I guess we'll never know which one came first."

"Sure we'll know," said Wanda, "because it says it right here: the area was named after him. We absolutely know."

"It's no longer called Farnsworth Landing, but Farnsworth Avenue is still the name of the main street," I added.

"That's a nice connection to the city's past," said Wanda. "Now in 1717, a man named Joseph Borden bought a lot of that land and changed the town's name to Borden's Towne.

He created a packet line of ships that sailed from Philadelphia to Bordentown. Travelers would then stop and rest in Borden's Towne and continue by stage coach to Perth Amboy. Then they would take a ferry to New York."

"They should have just taken the NJTRANSIT River Line train from Bordentown to Trenton and then hopped on a Northeast Corridor train to New York," said T-Bone. "That would be much faster."

"I don't think that would be faster," I laughed.

"Of course it would," he insisted. "Trains are definitely faster than stage coaches. Everyone knows that."

"Really?" I asked. "Are trains that *didn't* exist faster than stage coaches that *did* exist?"

"Good point," he said, turning red.

"It also says that most of the nation's Founding Fathers passed through Borden's Towne as it was a busy, colonial city," she continued.

"Is Bordentown as big as other important cities, like Trenton, Newark, or Camden?" I asked.

"Newark is a little over twenty-six square miles, Camden is about ten square miles, and Trenton is about 8 square miles," said Timmy.

The room turned silent, and we all stared at my brother.

"I like maps," he shrugged. "Plus, I really want to be an ambassador, too."

"Okay, genius," I challenged, "how big is Bordentown?"

"It's about one square mile," he confidently answered.

While I'll never know the exact moment it happened, Timmy somehow went from being my annoying shadow of a kid brother to being a pretty cool kid. It was the type of metamorphasis you see on the nature channels. He was trying so hard to be part of the group, and his love of maps and biographies could definitely come in handy. If the Bordentown trip turned out okay, maybe we could use him for other trips and upcoming projects.

"Timmy, are you sure? One square mile? That's it?" asked T-Bone. "That's kind of small. They probably can't fit too many important things in one square mile."

"I wouldn't say that," Wanda warned. "I found a website called **walkthetown.com** and downloaded a book called *Look Up, Bordentown*. It's a guided walking tour, and it seems like Bordentown has had plenty of famous people."

Before we could finish, we realized how late it was and decided to wrap up. I offered to call my grandfather and set up a day trip while Wanda offered to finish the research. We were excited because this walking adventure would combine a historic New Jersey city and the roots of our first free public school. Plus, the walking part was great for fitness. When Wanda suggested we follow the walking tour, we all agreed. After all, using a route planned by someone else wasn't cheating; *it was just taking a shortcut!*

CHAPTER FIVE

"Nick, T-Bone's here," my brother, Timmy hollered, upstairs.

"Okay," I hollered back, trying to find my left sneaker.

"Nick, Pop is here," Timmy hollered again.

"Okay," I hollered back, still trying to find my left sneaker.

"Nick, Wanda is here," Timmy hollered once more.

"Stop hollering!" my dad hollered before I could answer.

I could say that Timmy was very excited about our day trip to Bordentown, but the truth was that we were all excited on the days we explored. Planning Garden State adventures by checking out websites, photo galleries, videos, and reviews was definitely fun, but there was nothing like getting out there and seeing places firsthand.

"Where should we start?" asked my grandfather as we searched for a parking spot.

"The walking tour starts at the Old City Hall, 11 Crosswicks Street," Wanda answered.

"There's a spot," Timmy yelled as he frantically pointed.

"Good job, scout," replied Pop.

The old City Hall was a brick building with a clock tower on top, and it was almost directly across the street from the Consolidated Fire House. There was a plaque dedicated to William F. Allen (1846 – 1915), who was born in Bordentown and was the designer of Standard Time.

"Hold on," T-Bone protested. "How can someone design time? Did he make hourglasses or sundials?"

"No," Pop laughed.

"Did he make calendars? Date books?" T-Bone continued.

"No, it wasn't anything like that," said Pop. "During the 1800s, there was often confusion when it came to telling time in America."

"I get that," said T-Bone. "I've been known to get mixed up when I'm using analog instead of digital. It's totally confusing when the hour hand is in between two numbers."

"No," Pop shook his head and laughed. "They had to know how to tell time with analog because digital had yet to be invented. The real problem was that there were three kinds of time."

"Oh, I know this," said Timmy. "Past, present, and future."

"Wrong," I corrected everyone. "It's Eastern, Central, Mountain, and Pacific. Oh wait, that's four."

"Still wrong," my grandfather laughed. "There was natural time, local time, and railroad time. Natural time was using the sun's position in the sky, and local time was the time each town used, and there was usually a town clock to represent that time. And then, there was railroad time. There was a problem, however, because railroad lines kept time based upon where the line started."

"That sounds even harder than using analog," said T-Bone.

"It could be very confusing," Pop agreed. "Imagine waiting for a train in Chicago, on Chicago time, and the train you're waiting for is still on New York time."

As it turned out, Mr. Allen was the Secretary of the General Time Convention, and as a result of his dedication to create a standard time, the United States was divided into four time zones: Eastern, Valley, which became Central, Mountain, and Pacific. Before this convention, over eight thousand towns were all using their own local time!

"I'm glad they dedicated the clock to Mr. Allen," said T-Bone. "Although a giant digital clock would really be a good idea."

"Or a better idea," my grandfather laughed, "might be to learn how to tell time both ways."

We continued past Temple B'nai Abraham. In 1918, the Bordentown Hebrew Association purchased the double house and converted it to a synagogue. It looked like an ordinary house until you got close and saw the beautiful, stained-glass windows.

Across the street was St. Mary's Roman Catholic Church. The parish was formed in 1831 by Irish immigrants who were building the Camden and Amboy Railroad and the Delaware and Raritan Canal. First, they met at houses, then a simple meeting house, and finally, in 1870, the cornerstone for the church was set.

By definition, Bordentown City was technically a city, but it had a small-town feeling. There were colonial-style houses scattered in between churches, firehouses, shops, and restaurants. I was sure the kids who lived there now loved it as much as the kids who lived there in the 1700s. As we walked a little further, we passed the Clara Barton School.

"If I didn't know any better," said T-Bone, "I would have guessed this was a modern school."

"It is a modern school," said Wanda. "This is one of the elementary schools in the Bordentown Regional School District. That big school across the street, MacFarland Intermediate School, is also part of the district."

"I'm confused," said T-Bone.

"Analog time again?" asked Timmy.

"No," said T-Bone. "But how can one city be regional?"

"Bordentown City, Bordentown Township, and Fieldsboro create the district," my grandfather explained.

There was a large stone with a plaque in front of the Clara Barton School that honored Borden's Towne. We walked a little further and could see the Clara Barton Schoolhouse. I remembered how it was a ramshackle building when they gave it to her and realized how much work it must have been to fix it. Later, when it fell into disrepair, the children of the state restored it. It was surrounded by a white picket fence and was red brick with red shutters. When we peeked inside, we saw a furnace, chalkboard, benches, and a large desk. There was even a cardboard cutout of Clara Barton.

"Is that what your school looked like?" T-Bone asked Pop.

"Yes," he said sarcastically. "I'm a graduate of the class of 1826. I sat three seats away from Abraham Lincoln."

"Really?" T-Bone shrieked. "You knew Abraham Lincoln?"

"No, I didn't know Abraham Lincoln," my grandfather shook his head. "How old do you think I am?"

"Never mind," said T-Bone, wishing he could take it back.

We walked up to the Gilder House and then headed to 18 East Union Street for the library. After checking out the library, we headed to Farnsworth Avenue, which looked like part of a Christmas village or a snow globe. There were churches, bakeries, a deli, unique shops, and restaurants. Pop had been to all of them, from the Farnsworth House and Toscano's to Oliver's, Under the Moon, and Marcello's. He told us these were some of the finest restaurants he knew. We weren't sure where we would eat until we stopped in front of Jesters. They had inside and outside dining, which I loved, and our server, Anna, quickly greeted us with a smile. We must have been hungry because no one left a morsel on their plates. We ordered chicken tenders, burgers, and wraps. Everyone loved everything. There was something very exciting about sitting outside while you eat, especially in Bordentown.

"What happened?" I asked, pointing across the street to the enormous old bank building. "Wasn't that the ice cream place *I Scream, You Scream*? I loved that place."

"Yup," said Pop. "But now it's a restaurant called The Vault. Remember, in the old days, that beautiful building used to be a big bank, and now it's a fantatsic Italian restaurant. They serve traditional Napoletana-style pizza from a wood-fired oven, which is imported from Naples, Italy, and is handmade from crushed lava rocks. Their pizzas are carefully baked at nine hundred degrees for sixty to ninety seconds."

"Sixty to ninety seconds?" asked Timmy. "Is it like a giant microwave? Or a pizza volcano?"

"No, no, not at all," my grandfather laughed. "It's a beautiful oven that reaches such hot temperatures, you end up with a crispy, yet chewy, crust. You'll love it."

"We will?" I asked.

"Sure," he answered. "We're going there for dinner."

"Really?" asked Timmy.

"Sure," Pop replied. "But we have to do a lot of walking to work off our Jesters lunch before we have Vault pizza!"

We continued down Farnsworth Avenue, reading the bright blue flags that hung on lampposts. Each told about a different person or organization that helped shape Bordentown, the state, and the country.

Soon, we came upon 154 Farnsworth Avenue. It was the home of Thomas Paine, a founding father of the United States, often referred to as the *Father of the Revolution*. The only house and land he ever owned in America was this house and the seven acres of land he purchased in the early 1780s. Unlike George Washington, who was a general in the Continental Army, Thomas Paine's most important contributions weren't his time on the battlefield, they were his writings. In 1776, he wrote *Common Sense,* which was a call to arms for Americans. In 1776-1777, he wrote *The American Crisis,* which included the very famous phrase, '*These are the times that try men's souls.*' He was a talented writer, who used plain language and persuasive writing to explain the ideas of revolution to everyone from farmers to lawyers.

Right down the street, at 101 Farnsworth Avenue, we came upon the home of Francis Hopkinson. He represented New Jersey at the Second Continental Congress and is one of the five New Jersey men who signed the Declaration of Independence.

"Do you realize how brave the signers of the Declaration of Independence were?" asked Pop.

"Signing their names on a piece of paper made them brave?" asked Timmy.

"When you sign your name on a document that tells the country with the most powerful military that you want your freedom," I explained, "that makes you brave."

"When you sign it, knowing it will force a war," said Wanda, "that makes you very brave."

"And when you sign it," said T-Bone, "knowing that in the likely event your small, untrained army loses against that military giant, you'll be charged with treason and probably die, that's extremely brave."

"Well, I guess you knew," Pop laughed.

"Holy moly!" T-Bone exclaimed as he turned around. "That is the absolute biggest picture of Ben Franklin I've ever seen in my life!"

When we all turned around, we could see the enormous painting that covered the entire side of the Farnsworth House restaurant.

"That's not Ben Franklin," said Pop.

"Sure it is," T-Bone insisted. "It has to be Ben Franklin. It's an old guy with long, gray hair and a colonial outfit. It's not Washington or Jefferson, so who else could it be?"

My grandfather laughed and explained that the gentleman on the side of the building wasn't a Founding Father but the founder of Bordentown.

"Oh, that's right. It's Joseph Borden," T-Bone announced.

"No," Wanda excitedly shook her head. "That must be Thomas Farnsworth. He founded the town and, after all, this is the Farnsworth House."

"Hey, this name sounds familiar," I said, pointing to a blue flag up ahead.

"Joseph?" asked T-Bone. "It probably sounds familiar because it's a very common name in America. You can also say Joe, Joey, Jo-Jo, Joey-Pot-Pie...."

"No," I interupted, pretty sure T-Bone never knew a Joey-Pot-Pie. "Bonaparte! I'm talking about Bonaparte."

"Nope," he shrugged. "Never heard of him."

As I read the flag, I realized why it sounded so familiar. Joseph Bonaparte was the brother of Napoleon Bonaparte. It explained that he was Napoleon's older brother and the exiled king of Spain. In 1816, he bought large tracts of land from Trenton to Bordentown and then built a mansion overlooking the Delaware River. He lived there for twenty years and hosted many important visitors.

"He had a very colorful career," said Pop. "Napoleon was the emperor of France and he made his older brother, Joseph, the king of Naples. During Joseph's short, two-year reign, he made some progress bringing the backward country into the modern era and introduced educational reforms."

"Naples?" T-Bone gasped. "I wonder if he ate pizza from a volcanic oven when he lived in Naples."

"Even better," said Wanda, "we know he valued education."

"Good point," I agreed. "And since they both lived in Bordentown, he probably talked a lot about education with Clara Barton. Those must have been some conversations."

"Indeed," said my grandfather. "They would have been *some conversations*, given that he died in 1844 and she arrived in Bordentown in 1852!"

"Don't worry, Nick," said Timmy. "Easy mistake. But if you're nice, and I become an emperor, maybe I'll make you a king someday."

"Sure," I nodded, "when you become the emperor of France, you can make me the king of the country of your choice."

During our walk along Farnsworth Avenue noticed a war memorial. It listed the names of Bordentown residents that died during every war, starting with the Revolution. It was an honor to read those names, but it also showed what a contribution Bordentown made. Once we crossed Park Avenue, we came across some very big houses. When we reached Prince Street, we found the statue of Thomas Paine, or as T-Bone referred to him, our Revolutionary Neighbor.

"This is a great statue," I observed. It said *Father of the Revolution* along the bottom, and his pose was so lifelike. With his foot perched upon a rock, a book in one hand, and his other hand outstretched, I could see why he was so convincing. Even his statue was persuasive.

We headed down Prince Street and made a right on Park. My grandfather told us that the NJTRANSIT River Line station was just ahead as well as the Delaware River. The road dipped steeply so we would be at water level. There were still some boats bobbing along the docks and two meandering down the river. It was very quiet, and we watched an older gentleman throwing some bread to the birds. As we turned around and headed back up the steep incline, we heard a two-car River Line train pulling in. As quickly as it arrived, it was gone just as fast. The people on the platform who had been eagerly awaiting its arrival were quickly replaced with commuters returning to their cars.

We headed back to Farnsworth Avenue, this time to walk the other side of the street. My mom would have loved all of the unique shops, which meant my dad would have hated them. We stopped in The Old Book Shop, and I realized why I would never love digital books as much as I loved real books: *it was the smell.* I loved the smell of books. If smart had a smell, this would be it. Thankfully, there was no *Book Smart Aftershave* or T-Bone would have bought a barrel of it.

We checked out stores that were boutiques, and stores that sold antiques. There was an ice cream shop and a great deli called the Corner Deli. Even the drugstore was very unique, with a huge, old-fashioned sign out front.

One of our favorite stops was The Cake Box by Neelma. As soon as we walked in, we could smell the aroma of fresh-baked cupcakes. I liked that it was a family business, and I really liked the backyard patio. I scanned the glass cases. There were so many choices, and I realized we would need to return several times to try everything. By the time Pop paid for our cupcakes, they were almost gone.

"I guess you liked them," he laughed. "Well, that should keep you going until it's time for dinner, although next time I'd recommend eating them instead of inhaling them!"

We continued exploring, and soon we were ready for dinner. We arrived at The Vault, and it smelled amazing. I tried to subtly glance at what other people were eating. I wanted to try it all. They had some appetizers, salads, and even pasta, but we all wanted to try this pizza my grandfather had told us about. Since they were individual-size pizzas, Pop suggested we try four different kinds. Our waitress, Sabrina, suggested a Marinara, which was plain, a Margherita, which had fresh mozzarella, a Roni, topped with pepperoni, and a Sal Zeechee, topped with sausage.

The pizza tasted as amazing as it smelled, and there was no need for a take-out container; every piece happily disappeared. As we ate, I tried to picture The Vault as the bustling bank it once was. I figured the tellers never imagined their bank would become a restaurant. Then I thought about all of the places we go to and how I never imagined any of them them closing or changing. While I was never a big fan of change, my move from Philadelphia to New Jersey taught me that sometimes change can be good, *really good*.

I looked at every person seated at our table. I wondered if any of us would go on to do amazing things, the kind of things kids would learn about in one hundred years, or even two hundred years. Bordentown had inspired me. Learning about the achievements of people like Clara Barton, Thomas Paine, and Francis Hopkinson made me believe that one day Wanda, T-Bone, and I could also make important contributions to the world.

And of course, if Timmy became an emperor, he might even make me a king!

CHAPTER SIX

The next morning, I was inspired. I didn't sleep very well because I couldn't turn off my brain. I had so many ideas. I wanted to join T-Bone's stand for public schools, not just as his friend, but as his partner. I also wanted to do something to put books in the hands of kids who didn't have books. My mom always said readers are lifelong learners. I wasn't sure how a few kids could make a big difference, but I was determined to try.

I went downstairs to the computer and saw an e-mail from Billy. He had forwarded several letters he had received from the **nickyfifth.com** website. Each one was a suggestion of places we should visit, and each one was from a kid. Some were for places we had already visited, some were for places we had talked about visiting, and some were for places we had never heard of. Of course, we would read them all.

After a good half hour, I wondered why my house was so quiet. I looked at the clock. It was only 6:00 am. Since it was Sunday morning, I knew no one would be awake for a long time. At least that's what I thought. Soon, I heard a faint tapping on the window. I didn't see anything. Then I heard it again. Tap, tap, tap. I looked up once more and, at the front window, with his face pressed up against the glass, stood T-Bone. I turned off the alarm and slowly opened the door, trying not to make any noise.

"What are you doing?" I asked. "It's six o'clock in the morning."

"Six o'clock Eastern Time," he corrected me.

"Obviously," I said, shaking my head. "So what are you doing?"

"I couldn't sleep," he explained. "I've been up all night. Bordentown inspired me, and I have so many ideas! I wanted to sneak out at two o'clock in the morning, but I didn't wanna scare my mom."

"So you snuck out at six?" I asked, wondering if that was really any better.

"Sure," he said. "Six o'clock in the morning is the beginning of a new day. Two o'clock in the morning is still last night. I'd never sneak out at night. Plus, I left her a note."

"I have to admit it," I confessed, "I didn't sleep well either. Our visit to Bordentown inspired me, too."

"I know," he nodded. "I'm more determined than ever to take a stand for public schools."

"Me, too," I announced. "I'm totally in."

"So am I," said a familiar voice near my front door.

"Wanda?"

"I saw the lights on, and your door was half open," she explained. "Then, I heard you talking."

"You saw his lights and heard us talking all the way from your house?" T-Bone asked in amazement.

"No, I couldn't sleep, so I went for a walk," she said through a yawn. "When I saw your door half open, I was gonna close it. As I got closer, I could hear T-Bone."

"Let me guess," I laughed. "You couldn't sleep either?"

"Not a wink," she smiled. "My brain…"

"Wouldn't turn off?" I interrupted.

"Exactly," she agreed. "Bordentown really…"

"Inspired you?" T-Bone interrupted.

"Exactly," she nodded through another yawn.

"So where do we start?" T-Bone wondered.

"I think we should be logical. Let's make a list," Wanda suggested. "We'll list all of the things we'd like to do and then think about how we'll get them done."

"Sounds good," said T-Bone. "Can we start with my stand for public schools? It's really important."

"Absolutely," Wanda agreed as she wrote it down.

"Remember what my grandfather told me? I was thinking about how all kids should have books at home," I said. "I'd like to take a stand for kids who don't have books."

"That's great," Wanda nodded while she added it to the list. "What else?"

"Well, we can't forget about New Jersey," said T-Bone. "We have to continue our ambassador work so people know how unbelievable New Jersey is and where to go."

"Like Bordentown?" I laughed.

"Exactly," he agreed.

"I have one," said Wanda, "but I'm not sure where we would even start. This one is really big and, from what I've read, it's really complicated."

"Start at the beginning," T-Bone confidently responded.

"This one is a little harder than that," she admitted. "It was something your grandfather said that really stuck with me."

"About Bordentown?" I asked.

"No," she shook her head. "It's about education and the books. What did your grandfather say, in his opinion, were the three things that most affect education?"

"Reading, writing, and math?" T-Bone guessed.

"Oh no, I remember," I said. "He told us it was parenting, priorities, and poverty."

"Exactly," she nodded. "And of those three, which two are the easiest to change?"

I started thinking, but Wanda was too excited and way too impatient to wait for my answer.

"The two easiest to change are parenting and priorities," she continued. "Anyone can make a decision to improve their parenting or their priorities, but the really hard one to change is getting out of poverty."

"Can't they just get a better job?" asked Timmy as he entered the room, rubbed his eyes, and sat on the couch.

"That's what so many people think," said Wanda. "There are so many myths about poverty, and sadly, it's the biggest obstacle to improving education for everyone."

"What are the myths?" asked Timmy. "Is it a poverty dragon that breathes fire? Or a poor princess stuck in a tower?"

"They're fairy tales," T-Bone laughed.

"Oh," Timmy sighed. "Then what are the myths? I wanna learn about them, too."

Normally, I would tell my shadow-of-a-brother to leave because we were working. In Bordentown, however, he didn't really bother me. And if we were gonna make a difference, we could use all of the help we could get. I decided to let him stay.

"Well," Wanda began, "some people really believe that people want to live in poverty."

"What?" T-Bone gasped. "Who would want to live in poverty if they didn't have to?"

"Some people think if you're poor it's just because you're lazy or you're not working hard," Wanda continued, "or that you just like to collect money from the government."

"Money from the government?" asked Timmy.

"Sure," I said. "I read about programs that help people when they don't have enough money."

"I'm still saving for a new video game," said Timmy. "Can I get the rest from the government?"

"No, Timmy, it's not for video games," Wanda explained. "These programs are for things like housing, medicine, and food - important things."

"Oh, okay," Timmy said, almost sounding disappointed. "That's nice that they're helping people."

"Well, I think we should do some research about poverty," said Wanda. "I want to learn more about it because it affects every part of life for those who are poor."

"Hold on," said T-Bone. "Has the government been helping people for a long time?"

"Sure," Wanda answered. "Why?"

"Because if the government has been helping people in poverty for a long time, and there are still so many poor people, maybe they're not giving them enough money."

"Or," I suggested, "maybe they need more than money. If you get less than or just enough to survive, how can you ever escape poverty? Maybe they need programs, too."

"Do they have programs, Wanda?" asked T-Bone.

"Yes, lots of them," she said.

"Then maybe they need better programs," I suggested.

"That's why we have to learn about poverty," Wanda concluded. "We really shouldn't say anything until we know what we're talking about."

"Good idea," said T-Bone and Timmy at the same time. Sometimes I wondered which one of us was his brother.

"Hey," I said, getting everyone's attention. "I almost forgot. We got an e-mail from Billy yesterday. And before you get excited, T-Bone, it's suggestions from other kids. It's not about the bill to name us Official Junior Ambassadors."

I needed to say that fast before T-Bone jumped to the conclusion that our bill was voted on, found out it wasn't, and then got down. We didn't have time for a *T-Bone Code*.

"Well, what do we have here?" my mom asked as she rubbed her eyes and slowly navigated the stairs. "Is this some sort of convention?"

We told her all about our Bordentown trip in great detail. She never stopped smiling, not even once. When I asked her why she was so happy, she told us she believed we were about to do something truly worthwhile.

"I don't know how worthwhile," I shrugged. "Three kids..."

"Four!" Timmy interrupted.

"I mean, four kids taking a stand for public schools, for books in homes, and against poverty?" I said, questioning her enthusiasm. "We're excited, but these are all really big things. *What can we really do?*"

"Do what you do," she replied. "Just do what you do."

"Huh?" asked T-Bone, as confused as I was.

"Do what you do," she repeated. "How did you get a state full of children and families excited about New Jersey?"

"We should become the *Unofficial Junior Ambassadors of Poverty*?" asked T-Bone.

"No," she laughed, "but you already have a great formula. You research places, learn about them, then you share what you've learned. You've taught so many kids and their families about New Jersey, and you've motivated so many families to take action and explore New Jersey."

"Go on," I said, still trying to follow her logic.

"Instead of limiting your work to amazing people, places, and history, do your research about what makes public schools great. Figure out how you can get books in the hands of kids who don't own their own books, and learn what real poverty is as opposed to what many people think it is. Then just share it with everyone."

"Just share it?" I asked. "They are such big issues. Shouldn't we do something a little more concrete?"

"Start a soup kitchen?" T-Bone jumped up.

"No, you don't need to start an actual soup kitchen. You're really underestimating the importance of sharing good information," she explained. "Changing opinions is the first step to creating change."

"Mrs. A.," Wanda said in her most serious voice, "do you really believe that we can change opinions? Really?"

"Without a doubt," my mom answered. "I suspect most people just aren't aware of many of the issues and what really causes them. I believe most people are basically very good and when presented with good information, they tend to do the right thing."

"Why is there so much misinformation?" I asked.

"Remember, I said most people are basically good," she continued. "Sadly, not all people have good intentions. Some are blinded by greed, power, and ambition. The people with the most power tend to influence the information everyone receives."

"I also think it's because some people are uninformed," added Wanda. "My dad told me people are so busy trying to keep their houses, feed their families, and get through the day that they don't have time to think about bigger issues."

"That's true," my mom agreed "but at the end of the day, we're all in this together, and you kids can make people stop and think about things they hadn't given much thought to. Imagine if you could make people, people who may have never given it much thought, look at poverty in a new light. Imagine if existing programs that do little to lift people out of poverty were replaced with programs that offered hope. Imagine if people who were hopeless believed that they could do better, that their children could do better. Imagine if senior citizens and young families didn't have to choose between medicine or groceries. Imagine if veterans were offered training and job skills when they returned home. Imagine if we actually helped people who suffer from mental illness instead of pushing them onto the streets. Imagine if there was an end to homelessness and hunger."

"I'm imagining," T-Bone said with his eyes closed tightly. "I'm imagining, Mrs. A."

"Great, who wants pancakes?" she said as she headed toward the kitchen.

"Wait," I yelled. "Where are you going?"

"To make breakfast," she smiled.

"But we need you," T-Bone pleaded. "You're as inspirational as Bordentown. Do you want to be our leader? We could hold our official meetings at The Cake Box by Neelma. If we meet once a week, we'd be able to try all the flavors in no time. What do you say? Wanna be our leader?"

"No thanks," she smiled. "I can take you to Neelma's more often, and I'll help when you need help, but believe me, you've got this. You kids can do this!"

"Okay, then there's one more thing, Mrs. A.," he said, "and it's really important. *Can I get extra syrup and a side of bacon with my short stack?*"

CHAPTER SEVEN

What Bordentown did to inspire us, my mom did to motivate us. For the next week, we gathered as much information as possible. To make things easier and avoid everyone doing the same work, we decided to divide the research. T-Bone took public schools, I took books in the home, and Wanda focused on poverty. Timmy wanted to help, so Wanda invited him to join her after *she lost rock, paper, scissors.* Suddenly, we were like a well-oiled machine, and things were really moving along.

In addition to the issues we were supporting, we still needed to find some great places to visit. Luckily, New Jersey kids had really stepped up, and we had piles of ideas coming in. After reading through the newest batch, we had a hard time deciding where we should go next.

One thing was true: every submission was interesting. Many were from places we had visited, and they brought back great memories. Akshita from James Madison Intermediate School wrote about Menlo Park and inventor Thomas Alva Edison, explaining his achievements and his challenges. Kian, from Cedar Creek School in Lacey Township, wrote about Smithville Village. That reminded me of the day T-Bone tried to arrange a romantic swan boat ride with Wanda. Unfortunately, she thought my parents should have the romantic boat ride. While Wanda rode with my sisters, Timmy and I rode with a very Code Orange T-Bone!

Noah, from Wayside School in Ocean Township, wrote about Asbury Park and the Stone Pony, a historic music club known for launching the careers of New Jersey's own Bruce Springsteen and Bon Jovi. He even wrote about watching his cousin's band and his dad's band play there.

Ryan, from the Peter Muschal School in Bordentown, wrote about one of our favorite places, the Grounds for Sculpture. The indoor and mostly outdoor sculptures mixed art with the great outdoors. Seward Johnson, the founder, was brilliant for bringing the art outside. So many families with little kids probably skip museums because they're afraid their kids would be loud or run around. At the Grounds for Sculpture, you can run and make noise or just lay on a blanket under a shady tree.

Emma, of Greibling School in Howell Township, wrote a fascinating letter about the Old Ardena Schoolhouse, also located in Howell. As I read her colorful descriptions, they reminded me of the Clara Barton Schoolhouse and the beginning of public schools in New Jersey.

Two girls named Keyla and Veronica, students at John F. Kennedy School in Jamesburg, wrote about the Delaware River. It was an interesting choice, and they added many details, including General Washington's crossing on Christmas night, 1776, the turning point of the Revolution.

There was a letter about William Trent, founder of the City of Trenton and former owner of the Trent House, by Alison and Alexis, also of John F. Kennedy School. It was filled with interesting details and plenty of history; it was as outstanding as the house itself.

Allie, from Sharp Elementary School, was very busy and must have really loved New Jersey because she wrote about two different places in two different letters. The first was the Battleship New Jersey, one of our first Garden State adventures after my family moved from Philadelphia. The second was Ol' Barney, the Barnegat Lighthouse.

We needed to make some decisions about our upcoming day trips so I organized the letters into piles and told Wanda and T-Bone it was time. I even asked Timmy if he wanted to help us. I warned them it would be difficult. We had so many letters, and they were all great. I loved when kids painted pictures with their words. One of those was Lena Stein, from Old Farmers Road School in Washington Township. She wrote about a place we had never heard of called the Kenneth Lockwood Gorge, calling it the perfect mix of nature and history. After reading the story of a train accident on the trestle, we put the gorge on our list.

There was an idea from Shreya, a student at Irwin School in East Brunswick. She gave so many reasons for visiting Princeton, including comparing and contrasting it to other places. Adam, of Marlboro Elementary School, discussed the entire City of Trenton, one of our all-time favorite places. Reading what Shreya and Adam wrote reminded me of what Pop said about the roughly ten miles that separated one of the wealthiest towns in the nation, Princeton, from one of the poorest cities, Trenton. Even though we had already been to both several times, they were great choices, and we decided it was time to return.

David Dias, from Hamilton School in Harrison, knocked it out of the park. He wrote such an amazing piece about the Newark Museum, we couldn't wait to visit it. According to David, it was the largest museum in New Jersey, with over eighty galleries with art from all over the world. What really caught our eye was the Ballantine House, where you could see how the Ballantine family lived in 1885. Sounded like another New Jersey time machine to me!

Planning a trip was always the most exciting part of our job. That is, until the day we actually went on the trip; then that became the most exciting part.

"You know," Wanda said as she glanced at the places we selected. "Two of these cities have high poverty."

"Princeton and Trenton?" asked Timmy.

dad would make a big pile under the tree, and you would jump in. Then your older brothers would jump on you and not let you up."

"First of all," I began, "you know I didn't grow up in New Jersey. When I was little, I lived in Philly, and we didn't have trees or leaves. Second of all, if we did have leaves piled up and we jumped in, we would have cracked our heads open. We didn't have a front yard with grass; we had concrete. And third of all, I don't have older brothers. I'm the oldest kid in my family, so no one jumped on me."

"Oh," he said, giving it some thought. "Did you jump on Timmy and your sisters, or did your dad jump on you?"

"T-Bone, kids in the city don't jump in piles of leaves," I explained. "And, honestly, it sounds ridiculous."

"*Au contraire, mon frère*," he said in a bad French accent.

"What was that?" I asked.

"In French, it means on the contrary, my brother," he said with a giant smile. "It's so much fun. Watch this."

I couldn't believe T-Bone expected me to make a giant pile of leaves and jump in it like some sort of sugared-up toddler. Within ten minutes, he had an enormous mountain of leaves.

"This is where it gets fun," he exclaimed as he walked

backwards. "The key to a successful leaf leap is to get a long, running start."

He took off like a cannonball and soon closed in on the pile. Unfortunately, he tripped over a thick branch, which propelled him into the air. Rather than land gracefully, he dropped down like a sleepy bear that had fallen out of a tree.

"You were right," I laughed. "This is fun."

"Nick, Nick," he groaned from somewhere deep in the pile. "I think I broke my face."

I pulled some leaves off of the pile only to find T-Bone face-down. For a second, I thought he might have broken his face; or at least his nose. Luckily, he had only hurt his pride. As he emerged from the pile, George arrived. We looked like two little kids with their hands caught in the cookie jar.

Even though he was still pretty woozy, T-Bone managed to stand. Well, he stood for a second and then he dropped down on the ground. While George and I each grabbed an arm and pulled him up, T-Bone snapped out of it.

"What's going on?" asked George.

"Well, I'm not a doctor," I laughed, "but I think he landed too hard and got up too quick."

"Tommy, are you okay?" asked George.

"Unfortunately, it may sound good *to* you, but it isn't good *for* you," he continued. "Sure, this country needs doctors, lawyers, teachers, accountants, and all of the other jobs that make a college degree necessary. But don't forget that there are so many important jobs that require different skills."

"Like what?" asked T-Bone. "Because I'm pretty sure most schools want all kids to go to college."

"Like plumbers, carpenters, mechanics, truck drivers, painters, bricklayers, electricians, and the many other occupations that keep this great country moving and growing," he explained. "When we give kids the message that college is the only choice, we devalue our tradespeople and the good people who have other types of jobs."

"What do you mean by devalue?" I asked.

"If we place all of the value on college, that leaves less value for careers and jobs that don't require college," he said. "When students graduate from high school, they should be prepared for the path they choose, and they should be proud of their choice. Sometimes we make people who didn't go to college feel like they aren't as good as college graduates."

"So you really don't think everyone should go to college?" I wondered.

"Let's take a field trip," he said, reaching for his keys.

"Are we going to the zoo?" asked T-Bone. "Or the Old Barracks? Please say the Old Barracks; I love that place."

"Not that kind of a field trip," said George. "Hop in, and I'll show you."

We hopped in his car and headed out of his neighborhood.

"See that truck?" he asked, pointing to the Acme truck ahead of us. "Without truck drivers to drive those big rigs, we wouldn't have any of the items we need."

"Sure we would," said T-Bone. "We'd just go to the store."

"The stores would be empty if those trucks didn't roll out every day delivering food, furniture, clothes, and everything else we need to live. Look over there; do you see that mail carrier? She's delivering mail. Imagine if the U.S. Postal Service just stopped; think of all the things that we send and receive. Thanks to all of those postal workers, for the price of a stamp, a letter can travel across the entire country to its destination. That's a service and bargain that I'm afraid we take for granted."

"George, I never thought about it that way," I admitted. "But you raise some good points."

As we continued driving, George was far from done. He pointed out a strip mall filled with stores. Each store employed sales clerks and people who stocked the shelves.

There was a barber shop next to a hair salon. There was an Italian restaurant with outside seating, and we could see the busy servers and hostess taking care of the crowd.

"Boys, see those linemen up on the poles? They provide a very valuable service. See that auto body shop? Another valuable service," he continued.

"That makes sense," I agreed. "If everyone had a college degree, who would fix colleges, or build colleges, or make cars to get to college? Who would fix roads, put out fires, and cut your hair? Is that what you mean?"

"Absolutely," he replied. "Schools should prepare students to enter the world as productive, contributing citizens and provide an opportunity to pick the path they choose."

"Should anyone go to college?" asked T-Bone.

"Of course," said George. "There are plenty of jobs that require higher education. I just think schools should offer students a variety of options and then let them decide."

"That's exactly what my grandfather told me," I said.

"Smart guy," George nodded with a smile.

"What about the happiness thing?" asked T-Bone.

"Well, you can never fully appreciate happiness if you've

never been unhappy," he began. "When parents try to protect their kids from everything negative in the world, they're not preparing their kids for life. We learn more from failure than from success. Unhappiness is a great motivator, and boredom inspires creativity. When I was a boy, we invented our best games when we were bored. You know what we did when we failed?"

"Cried?" asked T-Bone.

"No, we didn't cry," he shook his head, "we tried harder. And if we failed again, we kept trying. It made us strong."

When we returned to George's, we had a whole new perspective about education and life. I couldn't wait to ask my mom what she thought about his ideas. As soon as we finished raking, George called me into the garage. He showed me boxes of books and told me they were books Martha had collected. He said as soon as I created a program to give books to kids, I was to come and take them. Knowing her cherished books were in the hands of kids who didn't have any books would have made Martha very happy.

When I walked out of the garage, I was feeling good, but I didn't see T-Bone. Suddenly, as I was about to call his name, I heard some rustling from a new pile of leaves.

"Nick, Nick," he grunted. *"I think I broke my face. Again!"*

CHAPTER EIGHT

While our lives continued to be hectic, Wanda somehow managed to plan a trip for Princeton and Trenton. Even though we had been to both several times, Shreya and Adam wrote such nice pieces about each one that we decided to return. Now that we were thinking about books, public schools, and poverty, we wanted to explore both places differently than we had in the past. This time, we would be less tourist and more social scientist.

The day of our trip, Pop and Wanda arrived at the same time. Timmy and I were already downstairs waiting for them. T-Bone, usually the first to arrive, walked in last. His aftershave smelled stronger than ever. I figured he was late because it took so long to baste himself.

"I think we should start in Princeton, then head to Trenton," Wanda suggested. "Then, if we follow Route 206 South, from Nassau Street in Princeton through Lawrenceville, we'll arrive at the Battle Monument in Trenton."

"Sounds good," said Pop.

"Do you know exactly where we're going when we get to Princeton?" I asked.

"No," she smiled. "I have no idea."

"Wait, you don't know what we're gonna do?" asked T-Bone, a little confused.

"Did you at least plan our Trenton trip?" I asked.

"Nope," she smiled again.

"I don't mean to be nitpicky or petty," said T-Bone, "but exactly what did you plan?"

"Not a thing," she shrugged.

"Madame co-President, may I have a word with you?" T-Bone asked as he motioned for her to join him in the kitchen.

While T-Bone headed toward the kitchen, Wanda never moved from the couch. After two minutes, T-Bone returned.

"Madame co-President, when I do this with my head, it means you are supposed to follow me," he said, wildly shaking his head.

"No thanks," she said as she shook her head and made the I-just-ate-a-lemon face.

Even though we knew she was just teasing him, it was pretty funny watching him shake his head and point to the kitchen. I knew exactly why Wanda wasn't moving; she absolutely hated when he called her *Madame co-President*. For some reason, T-Bone hadn't picked up on that one yet.

"Okay, then I'll ask you in front of everyone," he said in his most exasperated voice. "Wait, hold on. Now I forgot why I wanted you to come in the kitchen."

"You wanted me to come in and ask me, in private, why I don't have anything planned," she said with a giant smirk. "Am I getting warm?"

"How does she do that?" he asked, looking at me and Pop.

Pop and I were loving every minute of this conversation, even if it wasted a little bit of our trip time. T-Bone folded his arms and looked as if he was going to lose his temper. When he leaned in closer, he must have gotten a whiff of Wanda's shampoo. He stopped, looked at her, then told her never mind.

"If you must know," she began, "I thought we should let this trip just happen. I thought it would be nice to wing it."

"Wing it?" asked T-Bone, his nostrils beginning to flare

again. "We don't wing trips. We are New Jersey's Unofficial Junior Ambassadors. We don't wing things. We make plans. We have an itinerary. But we don't wing things."

"I think winging it might be fun," I agreed.

"I don't even know what winging it means, but it sounds like fun," said Timmy. "Does it mean we get to fly?"

It was the first time I had ever seen T-Bone this annoyed with Wanda. As far as I knew, in T-Bone's eyes, Wanda could do no wrong. I thought it was funny that this was the one thing that really upset him.

"I think we'll be just fine," said Pop. "It'll be interesting to see where the wind leads us."

Without Wanda reading off an itinerary, our drive started off pretty quiet. Luckily, T-Bone got over his fear of winging it and went back to being his usual T-Bone self. We arrived in Princeton, and the town was bustling. Even though it was a weekend, the campus was crawling with students walking, riding bikes, and some were even kicking a soccer ball. The restaurants seemed packed, and the stores were filled with customers carrying fancy shopping bags. As we walked down Nassau Street, directly across from the university, I started paying attention to all of the non-college people who made this college town run. If George had been with us, he probably would have pointed out every single one of them.

"I love this town," said a more relaxed T-Bone. "It just oozes with history."

"It's leaking history?" asked Timmy.

"It's not leaking," I corrected him. "It means really historic."

"I agree," said Wanda. "It's an amazing university and an amazing town."

"You know, Princeton and Trenton have something very important in common," I said.

"Oh, that's right," said T-Bone. "They both end in –*ton*."

"Besides that," I laughed. "They were both a part of the turning point of the Revolution. Don't you remember? In 1776, the British were winning the war. General Washington knew if we didn't win the Battle of Trenton, the war would have been over."

"Of course I remember," said T-Bone. "The Continental Army won the Battle of Trenton on Christmas night 1776 and then they won the second Battle of Trenton, and oh yeah, that's right, then they won the Battle of Princeton. Good one, Nick."

"Maybe we should do a compare and contrast between both Trenton and Princeton," Wanda suggested while searching on her tablet.

"Good idea," I agreed. "They both played an important role in the founding of our nation."

"I have one," said T-Bone. "Each one houses something very important to our state."

"The Delaware & Raritan Canal?" I guessed.

"Actually, that is something they have in common, but I was thinking of something that they each have that is unique, important, and historic," T-Bone gave more clues.

"I give up," said Timmy, never a fan of long guessing games.

"Trenton houses the State House and the massive capitol complex," said T-Bone.

"That's true," said Pop. "Trenton does house a massive capitol complex, with over two hundred office buildings, sitting on downtown, waterfront, prime real estate."

"Trenton is lucky," said T-Bone. "What an honor."

"Well, there are a couple of ways you can look at it," said Pop. "It's definitely an honor, but it's also a burden."

"How can being cool enough to be the capital be a burden?" asked T-Bone. "You know, on a map of the United States, only fifty cities get the stars, and Trenton's one of them."

"Trenton is a celebrity?" Timmy asked. "Is it like a movie star?"

"Well, the reason it can be a burden," Pop began, "is that Trenton's population is about 85,000 people. On weekdays, that number swells to over 135,000 people when you add the government workers, visitors, and protesters."

"Protesters?" I asked.

"Of course," Pop smiled. "A big part of a democracy is the opportunity for citizens to voice their opinions. Since the State House is where the governor and lawmakers work, this is where people voice their opinions."

"I'm still not sure how being the capital is a burden," I said. "Shouldn't Trenton be oozing capital money?"

"Okay," my grandfather thought for a moment, "picture a pie that's cut in four pieces."

"Apple or cherry?" asked T-Bone.

"It doesn't matter," Pop replied.

"It kinda does," T-Bone continued. "I haven't had cherry pie in a long time. Can we go with cherry?"

"Okay," Pop sighed. "Imagine you have a cherry pie cut in four pieces. Even though the whole pie is Trenton, one of "those four pieces is actually all of the land occupied by the state's capitol complex. Got it?"

"You mean the State of New Jersey sits on 25% of Trenton's land?" I said, quickly converting cherry pie to a percentage.

"Yup," Pop nodded. "And government buildings don't pay taxes to the town that houses them."

"Then thank goodness there are so many schools, parks, hospitals, and churches in the city," said T-Bone.

"Funny thing," said Pop, "schools, parks, and hospitals are part of the community, and they aren't taxed; neither are religious organizations, like churches."

"Wow," said Wanda, "I never thought about that. Trenton has so many schools, churches, parks, and hospitals besides the capitol complex. How do capital cities have enough money?"

"It's not easy," Pop explained. "What Trenton really needs is a PILOT from the state."

"Trenton has an airplane and no one to drive it?" asked Timmy.

"You don't drive a plane," I said, shaking my head. "You fly a plane. And I don't think he's talking about an airplane pilot."

"I'm not," Pop smiled. "I'm talking about a *Payment In Lieu of Taxes*. It just means that the state respects the amazing contributions made by the City of Trenton. It shows that they realize that hosting the capitol complex is a burden as well as an honor."

"Does the State of New Jersey provide a PILOT for the City of Trenton?" I asked. "Because if they don't, isn't it like having one of the poorest cities in the country supporting one of the wealthiest states in the country? Kinda unfair."

"Sadly, New Jersey has failed to recognize how much Trenton contributes to the state," said Pop. "It wasn't long ago that the city needed to fire over one hundred police officers because they couldn't afford to pay for them."

"But the capitol complex, those fifty thousand workers, visitors, and protesters, they use police, fire, and so many other city services, plus they use the roads and contribute to their wear and tear," said Wanda. "Isn't New Jersey the third-wealthiest state in the country while the City of Trenton is one of the poorest? This is so unfair. I'm going to write to the governor! Then I'm going to write to my state lawmakers! Then I'm going to write to my nana!"

"Your nana?" I asked.

"Yeah," said Wanda, "she's good at calming me down when I get all worked up. I called her after I learned about the whole Clara Barton story."

Wanda, with her new mission to attack poverty, was furious. She couldn't understand how things like this were just accepted. It was so clear that Trenton was being treated unfairly. Pop explained that life always seems easier when you're a kid. Things are either black and white or they're right or wrong; it isn't until we grow up that we understand how much gray there is. Wanda wasn't about to wait until she grew up. I could see the wheels spinning in her head. I had a feeling we would be doing a report about a PILOT really soon.

"So was Princeton the state capital, too?" Timmy wondered.

"No," I answered. "But both Princeton and Trenton served as the temporary capitals of the United States of America after the Revolution. And while Princeton was never the capital of the state, the governor works in Trenton, and the official governor's residence is in Princeton. First, it was Morven, and now, it's Drumthwacket."

"So was that the big thing they had in common?" asked Timmy, remembering T-Bone's original thought.

"No, no," T-Bone shook his head. "Princeton houses Princeton University."

"So Trenton has an Ivy League school, too?" Timmy wondered.

"No," I laughed. "Although Trenton does have Thomas

Edison State College; I think I know what he means. The capitol complex is massive and occupies a lot of Trenton's most valuable land, and Princeton University's campus is massive and occupies a lot of their land. That's a good one."

"Hmm, does Princeton University pay the town of Princeton a PILOT?" Wanda wondered, her wheels spinning even faster.

"Actually, Princeton University does pay the town of Princeton a PILOT," said Pop. "They recently entered into an agreement with the town. Some of the money goes to the public schools, some goes to first responders, and some goes to the town."

"Good to know," Wanda said as she scribbled something in her notebook. "Very good to know."

We continued walking, noticing different things than we usually did. We were looking at houses, not just the historic houses, but all of the houses. We saw very expensive cars, but also lots of people walking. We noticed the people, but we also noticed the great diversity. We saw people from every corner of the globe. I now understood why George used to spend so much time people watching at the mall. It really was interesting.

We walked around Palmer Square and grabbed some hoagies from Hoagie Haven. I remembered how amazing they were from our last visit. We squeezed onto a bench out front and savored every bite. A few minutes later, a woman pushing an enormous double stroller headed our way. There were two little girls, sitting side by side. They looked like they had just stepped off the cover of a kid's magazine. They were even holding hands. Alongside the stroller, however, was a little boy. Judging by my sisters' ages, he was probably about six years old. And unlike his sisters, he was loud. He was so loud, we could hear him half a block away. He wasn't crying; he was doing something my mom says is even worse. *He was moaning.*

"Mom, wh-y-y-y-y do I-I-I-I-I have to carry this heavy bag?" the little boy demanded. "You carry it."

"Because, sweetie," she said. "They're your new toys, and I'm pushing your sisters."

"You carry the bag and leave my *stisters* at the toy store," he suggested.

"Honey, I need you to cooperate with me," she pleaded. "Do you remember when we discussed the meaning of cooperation?"

"You carry this bag and give my *stisters* to someone else," he insisted. "Here, they can take them."

And with that, he grabbed the stroller and rolled it in front of T-Bone.

"Here, big kid, these can be your *ststers* now," he announced.

"Really?" asked T-Bone with a combination of surprise and excitement.

"No, not really," Pop said to T-Bone as he gently guided the stroller back to the frazzled mom.

"I'm so sorry," she said. "We just flew back from Colorado, and my husband is late meeting us. I think my son has a serious case of jet lag."

"Quite all right," said Pop. "By the way, it does get better."

"Do you know when?" she asked as the two sweet little girls started screaming.

"Not for a while," Pop smiled, "but eventually it does."

As she continued down Nassau Street, Pop turned toward the rest of us.

"How about we start heading to Trenton now?" he asked.

"Good idea," I agreed. "But I have a question. When you told that lady that it would get better, how did you know for sure? How do you know it won't get worse?"

"Because I raised a family," he said. "There are days when your kids are like angels and then there are days like that."

111

"I guess you're glad those days are over, huh, Pop?" I wondered.

"You might think so," he said. "But believe it or not, there are days that I wish I could wake up to the chaos of when my kids were little like that. That mom is frustrated now, but believe it or not, one day, she'll miss days like today."

On our way to the car, we headed toward the Princeton Battle Monument. It commemorated Washington's victory on January 3, 1777. It was massive. The front of the monument was very impressive; there was General Washington, leading his troops to victory. There was also the death of General Hugh Mercer. The north and south sides of the monument displayed the seal of the United States and the thirteen colonies. We noticed on the north side that there was an inscription: a skull and crossbones over the words -or *liberty*. The rear face of the monument had the following inscription:

> *Here memory lingers to recall the guiding mind whose daring plan outflanked the foe and turned dismay to hope when Washington with swift resolve marched through the night to fight at dawn and venture all in one victorious battle for our freedom.*

There were other smaller monuments and markers, and together, it highlighted the town's importance during the war. I started wondering if Princeton actually received enough recognition for its contributions during the Revolution. I also wondered if Mercer County was named after General Hugh Mercer. I assumed it was. We would be leaving the

Princeton Battle Monument and would soon arrive at the Trenton Battle Monument. Battle monuments, another thing they have in common, I thought.

When we reached the car, T-Bone went under his seat and pulled out a black, drawstring bag.

"What's that?" I asked.

"I kind of borrowed my brother's GoPro camera," he declared as he pulled it out of the bag.

"Kind of?" asked Wanda.

"Well, my brother, Teddy, was sleeping," T-Bone explained, "and I hollered in that I wanted to borrow his camera. I told him to say no if it was a problem, and he didn't answer."

"He was probably sleeping and didn't hear you," Wanda sighed.

"He didn't say *no*," T-Bone insisted. "So technically, he can't get mad at me."

"Yeah, sure," I laughed. "Your brother Teddy gets mad when you walk into a room. What do you think he'll do when he finds out you took his GoPro camera without asking?"

"I did ask," said T-Bone. "I think you mean what will he say *for taking it without permission.*"

"Tommy, how does it work?" asked Pop.

"Well, he has a lot of accessories, but I did find this head strap that the camera hooks on to," T-Bone explained as he placed it on his head.

Wanda and I looked at T-Bone, looked at each other, then burst out laughing.

"You look like a coal miner," I tried to say through the laughter.

"Keep laughing," he said. "We'll see who's laughing when I capture the whole ride from Princeton to Trenton."

"Hold on," Wanda stopped laughing. "That's not a bad idea."

"See," said T-Bone. "It's not a bad idea."

"No, taking it without your older brother's permission was a really bad idea, a terrible idea. But filming the ride to Trenton is genius."

"See, Nick, she called me a genius," he gloated.

"Okay, genius," I said. "From the back seat, how can you film anything other than the headrest in front of you?"

"I think we should tie T-Bone to the hood," said Timmy. "He could be a fun hood ornament."

While we discussed different ways to attach T-Bone to the hood, the roof, and the bumper, Pop took a more practical approach.

"Hold on," my grandfather said as he fished through T-Bone's drawstring bag. "Here's a suction cup that can go on the hood."

"Aww," said Timmy. "That's not as much fun as sticking T-Bone to the hood."

While Pop carefully mounted the suction cup and secured the camera, everyone began to get excited. I wondered why we hadn't thought of this before. Our reports would be so exciting if we videotaped our adventures and the rides to get there. Kids would have a bird's-eye view of what New Jersey really looked like. *Of course, it would be the bird's-eye view of a very low-flying bird.*

As we headed south on Route 206, also called Stockton Street in Princeton, we paid close attention to everything we were seeing. The houses were huge and included Morven, the former governor's mansion, and Drumthwacket, the current governor's mansion. Not only were these homes large, they were all very neatly landscaped. Many of them were set back from the street, and some were even gated. Except for traffic, it was very quiet. I hoped the camera was able to capture everything. T-Bone told us the lens wrapped all the way around, so it would film everything we saw.

As we drove past Morven, I remembered the funny stories Bill Byrne told us about growing up in that mansion. My favorite story was the one when protesters were on the front lawn with torches and his dad, Governor Brendan Byrne, went outside and did the simplest of all things…he sat down and talked to them. He didn't have the police arrest them or have the fire department douse their flames; he just listened to them and explained things. I wished things were more like that today.

We left Princeton and entered Lawrence. The name of Route 206 changed: now it was called Lawrenceville Road; there was even a stretch called Main Street. It was very similar to Princeton. As soon as we crossed over Interstate 295, we passed Rider University. I had been there once for a documentary about icebergs and how quickly they were melting. Somehow, we got turned around and couldn't find the building. At one point, I was positive we were walking in circles. I remembered a very nice student, Stephanie Eppolito, quickly helped us find our way.

Pop told us what a great town Lawrence was, and I could see why. There were so many mature trees and, like the houses in Princeton, most were set back from the road. I kind of liked that idea. Growing up in Philadelphia, we only had a small backyard. These kids were lucky; they had a backyard and a front yard.

"Lawrence's most famous Revolutionary War episode," said Pop, "involved the actions of Colonel Edward Hand before the second battle of Trenton in January 1777. It took place as the British and Colonial armies were passing from Princeton to Trenton. Colonel Hand's achievement is still celebrated every year with a march to Trenton from the Township Municipal Building."

"Your grandfather sure knows a lot about Lawrence."

"My grandfather knows a lot about New Jersey. Period," said Timmy, glowing with pride.

"Well, when you're as old as I am, you get around," Pop winked. "Did you also know Lawrence Township's original name was Maidenhead?"

"I didn't know that , but I do know they have Quakerbridge Mall and Mercer Mall," said Wanda. "My nana and I go shopping there sometimes."

"You're right," said Pop. "Quakerbridge Mall has undergone some beautiful renovations. It's one of my wife's favorite malls. Now when we get to the Brunswick Circle, if we were to go to the right, you would see the Colonial Lanes Bowling Alley. They have a modern facility, with neon lights, computerized bowling, an arcade, and laser tag."

"Can we go?" asked Timmy. "Please, please, bowling is my life. I need to bowl."

"Not today, kiddo," he said, "but definitely another day."

"But bowling, arcades, and laser tag are my life," he pleaded.

"I thought being an ambassador was your life?" I asked.

"Okay, okay. Being an ambassador, bowling, arcades, and video games are my life," he begged. "Can we please go, Pop? Please! I'll never ask for another thing. Never!"

"You know what, Tim," Pop said as he pretended to look on his phone. "They're closed."

I couldn't believe Timmy was actually falling for the same trick my mom uses on Maggie and Emma. She looks at her phone and tells them places are closed. In the beginning, she used to at least make it look real. After a while, she barely pretended to touch the screen. Just a quick glance at a dark screen was all she needed to trick my sisters. I couldn't believe anyone over seven years old could possibly fall for that old trick.

"That's a shame they're closed," said T-Bone. "It sounded like fun. Next time, we'll have to check their hours."

CHAPTER NINE

After the Brunswick Circle, things started changing from suburban town to city. In cities, houses are smaller, closer together, and closer to the street. People walked much more, use public transportation, and often gathered out front and on porches. Kids were running around and playing outside, and we could hear them laughing from inside the car. It reminded me of my old neighborhood in Philadelphia.

When we arrived at the Trenton Battle Monument, Pop reminded us again that it was only about ten miles that separated Princeton and Trenton.

We found a parking spot and walked over to the monument. It was closed, but we remembered so much from our last visit that we were able to tell Wanda all about it. Pop was impressed by how much we remembered and told us it was a remarkable symbol for the contributions made by the City of Trenton.

From the other side of the monument, we heard some voices. We stopped speaking for a moment and realized a group of business people were headed our way.

"Looks like we have company," one of the men said. "How are you folks today?"

"We're good," said T-Bone. "We're actually the Unofficial Junior Ambassadors of New Jersey."

"Hmm," the gentleman looked up as he cupped his chin. "Unofficial, huh? What does one need to do to become the Official Junior Ambassadors?"

"I wish we knew," said T-Bone, still annoyed that they never had a final vote for our bill. "We find, visit, and report on great New Jersey places. You'd think that would be enough."

"Let me ask you kids an important question," said the gentleman. "Have you written about the City of Trenton? You know it's the capital city, right?"

"We've actually done several reports about Trenton," said T-Bone. "Now we're comparing Trenton and Princeton."

"Oh, that's interesting," he nodded. "In my opinion, they have much more in common than people may think. Both are historic, very important, and they each have a unique tenant. Princeton has the university, and we have the State of New Jersey."

"We were just talking about that," I said. "My grandfather told us about the massive capitol complex. But we did see some differences, too."

As soon as I said it, I stopped myself. I was afraid to actually say some of the differences out loud. I was afraid of saying something inappropriate. I was hoping he would forget that I even mentioned the word differences.

"So tell me about some of the differences you observed?" he smiled.

"Well, I mean, not much, it was kind of like, you know, it's just, umm, but, yeah, they're almost the same," I stumbled through an awkward jumble of words. By the time I stopped talking, that sentence had absolutely no meaning.

"What my friend is trying to say," said T-Bone, "is that the towns have similarities, but they have differences, too. In Princeton, people looked like they were on the move. In Trenton, we saw some boarded-up houses and businesses, and some of the businesses looked like they were closed. It seemed like there was a little less hustle and bustle. You know what I mean, right?"

"I actually do know what you mean," he said with an assuring smile. "You see, there was a time when Trenton was all hustle and bustle. This is where doctors, lawyers, politicians, judges, legislators, and captains of industry lived. Trenton was a manufacturing giant. Places like West State Street and

Greenwood Avenue were some of the many streets filled with mansions. And just like Princeton, we were even the nation's capital for a brief time."

"What happened?" Timmy asked.

"Oh, he doesn't mean, what happened?" I tried to stop him from embarrassing everyone, praying he would avoid the words *poor* or *poverty*. "He just meant that it must have been nice back then."

"That's not what I meant," Timmy insisted. "I meant, what happened? Some parts look poor, and some parts don't."

"It's okay, son," he said. "It did change. It's not a secret. Like many cities across the country, times have been tough for Trenton and our residents. When manufacturing jobs left, many opportunities left, too. But you know what? Right now, we have a great opportunity to work together and make things happen."

"Do you ever think Trenton will get its hustle and bustle back?" asked Wanda.

"I do," he nodded. "You see, times change; we can't stop that. What we can do, however, is adapt to those changes. The greatest obstacle we have right now is poverty. If we can work together on poverty, other things will begin to improve. We may no longer have manufacturing, but we have many incredible assets like our people, the Delaware

River, a growing arts community, and amazing history."

"I agree. I think people are uncomfortable saying the words *poverty* or *poor*, so they just pretend it doesn't exist," said Wanda. "It's nothing to be ashamed of; my grandfather always tells us about how poor he was when he was a kid, and Nick's grandfather told us everyone he knew was poor. I don't think people should be judged by their money."

"You're right; it's nothing to be ashamed of," he agreed. "But fixing poverty, however, is not something that happens overnight. I believe if you get a group of good people together, people who are dedicated to solving a problem, that problem should be scared."

"Does Trenton have a group of dedicated people?" I asked.

"As a matter of fact, there are many groups," he smiled. "And thanks to Reverend Taylor's efforts, many of those groups have been working together to solve these problems."

"Who's Reverend Taylor, and what'd he do?" asked T-Bone.

"Well, he started the Capital City Community Coalition, a group that meets to discuss the city's problems and come up with solutions," he explained.

"Just out of curiosity, do they split the problems up?" Wanda wondered. "Or do they list them by priority and focus on the most important problem together?"

"Actually, the members discuss problems, and others offer solutions or assistance," he said. "The coalition includes folks like the Trenton Police Department, the Trenton Fire Department, the FBI, Homeland Security, the State Police, FEMA, the County Prosecutor's Office, colleges, religious organizations, health groups, and so many others. It's quite an interesting assortment."

"When I grow up," I announced, "I'm gonna go to one of those meetings and tell the problem solvers that kids in cities have one book per three hundred kids in their homes. Then I'll ask them to help me collect books and give them out."

"Why wait?" he asked. "I believe Reverend Taylor opens the meetings to everyone. You should go."

"Anyone can go? Even a kid?" I asked.

"A kid with a good idea should be welcome anywhere, don't you agree?" he said with a smile.

"I see some new houses," said T-Bone, noticing the new homes across from the monument. "They're really nice."

"Thank you," he smiled. "It takes time, but I think this is the beginning of a renaissance in Trenton."

"You mean you're going to have knights on horseback and jousting?" Timmy exclaimed.

"No," he laughed, "not a Renaissance Faire. This is more of a rebirth."

"Oh, that's a shame," said Timmy. "Because I like jousting."

"Me, too," said the gentleman. "Well, kids, I have to get back to my meeting. Enjoy your visit."

As they walked away, we looked at each other and realized we never got his name. Too bad, I thought, because he really seemed to know a lot about the city.

When they pulled away, T-Bone noticed the license plate.

"Hey, I guess that guy can never forget his license plate number, huh?" he said with a laugh.

As the vehicle drove past us, I realized why T-Bone was laughing. It had a number 1 in the middle of the plate and the word *Mayor* underneath. To me, the obvious conclusion was that we had just spoken to Trenton's Mayor Jackson. To T-Bone, however, the obvious conclusion was that we just met the guy with the easiest license plate in the world.

We decided to drive around and learn more about the people who lived in Trenton. We stopped at a park on Roebling Avenue. It had modern, silver benches and tables that looked like furniture for a rocket. We sat next to a nice family. The mom told us that she absolutely loved taking her kids to this park, but she couldn't do it as often as she'd like.

"How come?" asked Timmy.

"Well, my husband and I both work two jobs," she said with a smile. "We don't have much free time with our kids."

"Wait, that's four jobs," exclaimed T-Bone. "That's too much. Maybe you should give up things like designer clothes and luxury vacations so you can go down to one job each."

"Designer clothes? Luxury vacations?" she laughed. "That's a good one. It takes those four jobs just to keep a roof over our heads, food in their tummies, and shoes on their feet."

"Can you just pick a job that makes more money?" I asked.

"Well, I called the White House to see if they had any applications for First Lady, being that I love to get dressed up and have dinner parties for hundreds of people. Turns out, you have to be married to or taking care of things for the president. I called NASA to see if they had any astronaut openings, then I remembered how I get carsick. So as you can see, my options are a bit limited," she sighed. "I didn't go to college, I have two small children, my husband works crazy hours, and my mom is very sick."

"So you take care of two small kids and one sick mom, plus you have two jobs?" asked Timmy.

"That's right," she said. "But I'm not complaining. There are some folks who have it much worse."

Her kids were really cute, and she hardly took her eyes off of them. You could just see how much she appreciated every moment she got to spend with them.

I looked to my right and heard a soft whimper near a tree. There was a girl, probably around Timmy's age, who was sitting on the grass and crying. Before I could say anything, T-Bone was on his way over. I was hoping he wouldn't say anything stupid.

"What's wrong?" he asked.

She just looked up at him.

"It's okay," he continued. "You can tell me what's wrong. I'm T-Bone."

"Nothing's wrong, T-Bone," she said, lifting her tear-stained face in our direction.

"Well, I hate to argue with a stranger, but I think something is definitely wrong," he persisted. "Maybe you'll feel better if you talk about it."

"Fine, I'll tell you what's wrong," she said. "I miss my mom, and I miss my sisters."

"See, that wasn't so hard, was it?" he asked. "So tell me, are they on a vacation? Checking out colleges? At the mall?"

"Really?" she asked. "A vacation? Colleges? The mall? No, they said my mom couldn't take care of us, so they put us in foster care."

"Wow, that's rough," said T-Bone as he sat down next to her. "You and your sisters got split up?"

"Yup," she nodded. "I'm the oldest, and now I can't even take care of them or help my mom."

"You're right; that is terrible," he agreed. "That's the worst."

"Maybe we should try to cheer her up," I whispered.

"I don't think she can be cheered up," said T-Bone loud enough for her to look over at me. "Can you?"

She rolled her eyes just like Wanda did every time T-Bone spoke. I really liked this kid. T-Bone told her that even though we couldn't really help her, we could at least be friends. We talked to her for a while and realized how strong she was. She was living with strangers, in a strange house, going to a new school. She could have given up so easily, but she was determined to get her family back. I couldn't imagine dealing with such serious issues and being able to focus on schoolwork. I decided we should change the subject to something happier. Unfortunately, T-Bone had his own plan.

"Is your foster family awful?" he asked.

I immediately gave him a look to tell him that his question was totally inappropriate. Luckily, she didn't seem offended and started to answer.

"No," she shrugged. "They're okay. They're just not my family, that's all."

"Is this your first foster family?" T-Bone continued.

"No," she said. "I've had lots."

"Really?" I asked, kind of shocked.

"Really," she said.

"Were they all nice?" asked T-Bone.

"No," she hesitated. "Some were nicer than others. Some took me and my sisters together, and some didn't."

"Do you think you'll go back with your mom soon?" he wondered.

"Don't know," she said, never looking up.

Her name was Maya, and I felt bad about her situation. George had mentioned foster kids when we were raking his leaves, but I never met someone in foster care. Turns out, she was no different than any other kid; she just seemed sadder. Earlier, I thought I was lucky because I had books, but now I felt lucky just to have my family. I couldn't imagine how hard it would be to wake up in a new house with strangers. I respected Maya. In fact, I had a new respect for people who faced the challenges of poverty. It made everything harder and required lots of decisions to be made. That mom at the park had to make tough decisions. Even though she would rather be home with her kids, she knew they wouldn't have enough money if she didn't work her second job. Tough decisions, I thought.

We had been to Princeton and Trenton so many times that I thought there was nothing new to see or learn. I was wrong. I realized the most significant thing these two towns had in common was bigger than history and bigger than wealth and poverty. Both Princeton and Trenton had amazing people. Different lives? Yes. Different resources? Yes. Different experiences? Absolutely. But Princeton and Trenton were filled with good people, people trying to live their lives, trying to make sure their kids had what they needed. I remembered my baseball coach in Philly once telling us that a team is only as strong as its weakest player. He told us that to win, we needed to work together and help each other. Maybe New Jersey was like a big team. Maybe by helping those in poverty, we would be helping everyone, *the whole team*. Then I thought about a famous quote from Benjamin Franklin. He said that *an ounce of prevention is worth a pound of cure*. Maybe the work we put into preventing poverty would turn out to be so much less work than trying to help everyone who already lived in poverty.

I wasn't sure what the answer was, but I knew I had to do something. Now I just had to figure out what that something was. I decided to e-mail Reverend Taylor and ask him how we could get books to the kids in Trenton. Maybe he would have an answer.

The next day, I looked him up and sent that e-mail. I quickly received a response. He invited us to come speak at their next meeting. When I told my mom, she was really proud of us. When I told her it was on a Thursday morning, at first, she hesitated. After thinking about it for a moment, she said if it just involved missing a couple of hours of school, I should go. She called it a valuable learning experience, so I called Pop and told him the plan. He loved it and offered to take us. T-Bone immediately said yes, and Wanda confirmed after checking with her mom.

That Thursday morning, I was anxious to talk about the crisis facing kids in Trenton. I didn't know if anyone there could help, but I knew it was my job to convince them. When we arrived at the Friendship Baptist Church, I could feel my hands start to sweat. That was not a good sign. The meeting was held in a big room, and the tables were set up in a giant rectangle. There must have been forty people there. Suddenly, I forgot what I wanted to talk about. My mind was racing. I could feel sweat beading on my forehead. T-Bone and Wanda, on the other hand, were just as cool as cucumbers. They were calmly spreading cream cheese on their bagels, and T-Bone was talking to the members of the Trenton Fire Department. I was too nervous to eat.

Ten minutes later, Reverend Taylor called the meeting to order. This was a bad idea, I thought to myself. I started looking around the room for an emergency exit. I knew I didn't have a real emergency, but it sure felt like one.

"I received an e-mail from a young man explaining a crisis many of us probably didn't realize existed," Reverend Taylor began. "This young man wrote about the number of books children in suburbs have in their homes and the number of books city children have in their homes. Since we are here to solve problems, perhaps we can come up with a solution. Having said that, I'd like to invite Nicky Abruzzi to speak."

I stood up to talk and felt like I would faint. Why did I agree to do this? Did I forget all about my awful debates with T-Bone? My tongue felt like it was swollen, and my throat was bone dry. There was no way I could do this. As I stood there, looking down at the white tablecloth, I was paralyzed with fear. Slowly, Wanda slid a piece of paper in front of me. It read *say good morning, everyone.*

"Good morning, everyone," I said, barely lifting my head and avoiding eye contact.

As they smiled and said good morning, another piece of paper arrived. This time she wrote *introduce us.*

"My name is Mickey, I mean Nicky, and I'm here with my friends, Rhonda and Tommy, wait, I mean Wanda and Johnny, no, I mean Wanda and Tommy."

This was definitely not good. *Where was a fire drill when a guy needed one?* Unfortunately, it got worse. When I went to point at T-Bone, I knocked over a pitcher of water. I stood there, frozen with fear, as ice-cold water ran down my leg and through my shoe. Luckily, T-Bone and Wanda sprang into action. Instead of starting to panic because I was ruining everything, T-Bone and Wanda did what they do best.

"Good morning, everyone," said T-Bone. "You'll have to excuse my friend here; he isn't a fan of speaking to large groups. However, on the bright side, at least he only spilled water. If it was milk, we might all be crying right now!"

Everyone started laughing at his *don't cry over spilled milk* reference. I didn't know how he did it. He spent about five minutes explaining the crisis for kids in inner cities and then he introduced Wanda. She got up and suggested a book drive: an event where we would collect books and give them to the kids in Trenton's public schools. I didn't know how she did it either. She was so calm and sounded like a professional speaker.

Fire Captain Mike Burzachiello suggested we use the city's firehouses to collect books and use fire headquarters to organize them. The Mercer County Prosecutor, Angelo Onofri, Captain Veldon Harris, and Agent Marvin Johnson offered to collect books, too. Police Director Ernie Parrey said it was a great idea and offered to help. A team from FEMA Corps offered to help sort the books. Before we knew it, we had an official book drive underway.

While I sat there with a sweaty forehead and soaking wet shoes, my friends saved the day. The fire department even offered to deliver the books with fire trucks. I looked at my grandfather. He smiled, nodded, and gave me a big wink.

When the meeting was over, people were handing Wanda their business cards. Since we were in middle school, we didn't exactly have business cards. She just told them we would contact them.

"Fine job, kids," Reverend Taylor said. "I'm impressed."

"I'm sorry about the water," I said, still pretty embarrassed.

"No apologies," he laughed. "And as your friend stated, at least we're not crying over spilled milk."

"Thank you, Reverend," said Wanda. "We appreciate the opportunity to speak to everyone. I'll call the Board of Education and see how many books we need."

Wanda and T-Bone were amazing. In fact, everyone at this meeting was amazing. They were talking about chess tournaments and events where kids could speak to law enforcement officers about possible careers. I figured this was why Mayor Jackson was so hopeful. When a city faces hard times, it requires so many good people and good ideas coming together. I was really happy that we found out about the Capital City Community Coalition and even happier when Reverend Taylor called us *its newest members*.

CHAPTER TEN

The day after our coalition meeting, we were still so excited. I wasn't excited about my public speaking; that was terrible. I was, however, very proud that we were about to do something that could affect a lot of kids. As I walked from class to class, my mind was racing. The idea to give books to kids was basically my idea. I started to get really nervous. What if I failed? A million negative thoughts invaded my mind. One bad thought would pop up, and as soon as I calmed myself down, another one would pop up. I felt like I was playing mental whack-a-mole.

When I opened my locker, an envelope slid out. My name was on it, and I instantly recognized the handwriting. Besides slipping me secret cue cards during the meeting, Wanda had also taken plenty of notes for us. This envelope contained an entire plan for providing kids with books. Not only did she figure out how we would do it, she thought of every detail. The best part was on top of the page: Nicky Fifth's CODE READ.

Wow, I thought, she even gave my idea a great name. As I read Wanda's plan, I realized she had already called Captain Burzachiello and discussed how we could do everything. We would place big boxes at the firehouses. People would drop off books and then we would sort them, put them in bags, and bring them to the schools. I started feeling much more excited and much less nervous. It wasn't just because my idea turned into a program with a cool name, but because we really were a great team.

I headed over to Wanda's locker to thank her. As she opened the door, an envelope fell out.

"You even send notes to yourself?" I asked.

"Send notes to myself?" she sighed as she placed it on a stack of envelopes eight inches high. "They're from T-Bone."

"Why is T-Bone sending you notes? And why does your locker smell like T-Bone's aftershave?" I asked, recognizing the unique, yet overwhelming, aroma.

"I'm not sure," she shrugged. "They smell like him, and they're all about my hair. Do you know anything about this?"

"Not a thing," I quickly tried changing the subject. I knew Wanda was a human lie detector, and the more I denied knowing about T-Bone's feelings, the more she would figure it out. "Well, anyway, thanks for everything you did. I love the name CODE READ; it's pretty catchy."

"You have a good idea," she nodded. "I'm happy to help. My dad called his friends, Rich and Barb, at the UPS store in Bordentown, and they offered to donate giant boxes. We can stop by anytime. Seth and Jason will have them ready."

"That's great," I said, very relieved that Wanda was on our team. "Should we meet after school to talk about the Newark Museum and the Ken Lockwood Gorge?"

"Definitely," she agreed. "I have my binder."

After school, Wanda and I waited for T-Bone, who was probably dousing himself and a stack of envelopes with aftershave. When he arrived, I decided not to mention the stack of letters. Teasing him about Wanda could cause a Code Red, and I needed him to be at his best.

"Before we talk about the next trip or the books, I have to say something," he announced in a very serious tone. "I've been reading some articles and talking to more teachers. I'm not happy about all of this standardized testing. Shouldn't teachers be allowed to teach? Shouldn't we test the things they're teaching instead of teaching things that are on a test?"

"Absolutely," my mom agreed as she joined us. "You know, when I first started teaching, that's how it was. It was more personal and so much more enjoyable for the kids. Look, even adults have a hard time sitting through boring classes. Imagine kids with seven boring classes each day. That's what happens when you hand a script to a teacher."

"Scripts aren't bad," said Timmy as he walked in behind my mom. "Movie stars use scripts, and people always ask for their autographs. Maybe you'll become rich and famous."

"Teachers don't teach to become rich and famous," my mom laughed. "You become a teacher because you enjoy helping people learn. It's really not complicated. At least, it wasn't."

"I know," said T-Bone. "They're called teachers, not testers. We should outlaw tests!"

"Nice try," she said, "*but teachers aren't against tests.*"

"Hold on," T-Bone exclaimed. "Now I'm confused."

"There are some people who think teachers are afraid of tests, but that's just not true," my mom explained. "Tests are a valuable tool, but they're just one of many tools. Tests are bad if they become the most important tool."

"Imagine if you went to your doctor for a checkup and they only looked inside your ears," said Wanda. "That doesn't give the doctor a clear picture of your health."

"That would be awesome," Timmy nodded.

"How can you measure someone's progress with one standardized test?" I added. "What about homework, classwork, projects, and participation?"

"Exactly," my mom sighed. "The tests that big companies promise will make kids more ready for college and careers are creating a situation where students are less prepared than ever. I don't think most parents realize what's happening."

"Should we tell the coalition about it?" T-Bone wondered.

"The only real way to stop this madness is for parents to understand how it's affecting their children and for those parents to speak out," she explained. "When a whole school year is geared for one test, it's never good. When teachers aren't allowed to teach or be creative, it isn't good. We keep moving away from what's really important."

"Maybe teachers should tell people," T-Bone suggested.

"We do. We have. We are," my mom sighed. "But no one is listening to the teachers."

"I'm not an expert," I admitted, "but aren't teachers the exact people they should be listening to?"

"You would think," she said. "But look at what's happening in education. We've eliminated the arts in so many schools; we have larger classes and less aides. Some school librarians work at two and three schools, while many art teachers travel around on a cart. Many schools have made cuts to athletics, food service, and counselors. These things are important; they matter. We keep giving students and teachers less, yet we keep expecting more."

"Dad says when teachers try to explain what's wrong, some people say they're lazy and afraid to be evaluated," I said.

"Who said my mom is lazy and scared? I want to know," demanded Timmy. "You're not lazy and scared, Mom!"

"Thanks, Timmy," my mom smiled. "But, the truth is, teachers aren't afraid of fair evaluations for ourselves or our students. We sacrifice so much instruction time for tests that hardly measure our students. Then they take those results to measure whether we are doing our jobs."

"Maybe they should use an obstacle course," offered Timmy.

"They're not trying to see who's the fastest," said T-Bone. "I think it should be a *Teacher Bee*. It would be like a spelling bee, but there would be questions for all subjects."

"Or a mud run," added Timmy. "Or gladiator games. Or a hula hoop contest. That would be sweet."

"There are so many things that teachers can't control. How can they be solely responsible?" Wanda wondered. "Instead of standardized tests, maybe we should just send them to the Olympics. Judging teachers with gymnastics or a bobsled makes as much sense as what's happening now."

"Good one," I said, picturing my English, math, and science teachers sliding down a bobsled track.

"Again, it's really not that complicated," my mom laughed. "It's actually simple. Teachers should be evaluated on their teaching abilities by their administrators. Students should be evaluated by their own growth and progress. When students are struggling, interventions should be in place to help them."

"I've always thought about becoming a teacher one day," said Wanda. "But it sounds scary. What if you're a good teacher and you do everything you're supposed to do, but some of your students refuse to do their work? What if some of the parents don't make sure their kids are working hard? What if the school doesn't have the resources the students need? If I'm the teacher, *that's all my fault*? No, thank you."

"Wanda, you could never do anything wrong," T-Bone quickly defended her.

Instead of thanking him, Wanda gave T-Bone a major eye roll while Timmy made kissing noises.

"Sadly, Wanda," my mom continued, "so many talented, young people are not becoming teachers for that exact reason. It's also the reason that record numbers of talented, veteran teachers are leaving or have left. They see how the changes are hurting students and feel helpless."

"Okay, Mrs. A.," said T-Bone, "I've heard enough. How do I help? How do I take my stand?"

"Like I said before, Tommy," she said, "do what you do. "Knowledge is power. Use your voice to get people talking about what kids really need to succeed. Focus on the things you've been learning about: parenting, priorities, and poverty. That's what will change education and improve progress."

"Should we call the lawmakers in Trenton?" he asked.

"You should always reach out to lawmakers when you have something on your mind," she suggested. "I know a woman named June who is almost ninety years old, and she still writes letters to lawmakers whether she agrees or disagrees. She knows the value of her voice, and she's still involved."

"That's it!" T-Bone exclaimed. "I'm going to be like June."

"Okay," Timmy added. "I'll be like September because T-Bone took June, and July and August are way too hot."

I never realized how smart my mom was until we started having these discussions. I always knew she was smart, but now I realized just how smart. I liked how she was more interested in change than blame and decided that's how I would try to live my life, too. The problem, of course, was getting people to understand what was happening.

While T-Bone and I scribbled some notes, Wanda was researching the Kenneth Lockwood Gorge suggestion from Lena Stein. We all loved the idea of combining nature and history. Pop volunteered to bring us, and since we had never been there, we needed to plan this trip well. This was surely not a time to wing it.

The gorge was located in Hunterdon County between Califon and High Bridge. Wanda and I started Googling its location to see if we could visit the gorge and the Newark Museum on the same day. They were on two different sides of the state, but both in North Jersey. It looked like we could go to the gorge and then travel east along Interstate 78 to get to the museum. It was forty-six miles away, and we decided that with our very busy schedules and all of the stands we were taking, this would be the best bet.

After an hour, we had compiled all of our information. T-Bone was also finished taking notes and quizzing my mom. When we showed him what we had done, he smiled.

"I may have forgotten to mention something," he said.

"What's that?" I asked.

"I was afraid you might want to wing our trip to the Newark Museum," he explained, "so I called David Dias to ask him some questions."

"David Dias who sent the suggestion?" I asked.

"Yup," T-Bone nodded. "He's a really nice kid. He goes to Hamilton School in Harrison, right outside of Newark. He even offered to meet us there if we wanted a tour guide."

"Great idea," Wanda said with a smile. "See if he's available Saturday."

When Wanda turned around, T-Bone pointed to himself and mouthed the words *great idea* while wildly nodding his head.

By the time Saturday morning rolled around, everything was planned, and we were ready for a long adventure. Pop brought along a cooler with cold drinks and some snacks. We told David we would call him when we left the gorge. Since it was a long drive to the gorge, we decided to leave early, really early. Once again, T-Bone arrived in his great outdoors attire: an all-white outfit with his socks tucked into his pants and the orange hat. Just like last time, he looked like a safety cone on top of a snowbank or a giant bottle of glue. Luckily, my dad wasn't awake to see him.

It was a crisp, fall day, and the sun was shining. The air was starting to make me think of Thanksgiving, one of my favorite holidays. Since it was a Saturday, traffic was pretty light, and the drive was easy. Wanda described a family-friendly destination great for hiking, strolling, biking, and picnics. There were rock formations and endless paths. We might also see a black bear although that wasn't high on my list of things to see.

As we approached the gorge, the road wound up and down steep hills. At one point, I thought maybe we were somewhere we shouldn't have been. Pop must have felt the same way because as soon as we came upon two cyclists, he stopped and asked for directions to the gorge. The man and woman looked confused, so Pop repeated the question.

"The gorge," he said slower and louder. "Do you know how to get to the Kenneth Lockwood Gorge entrance?"

"Uh, this is it," the man said, pointing to the parking area right up ahead.

I wasn't sure, but it looked like Pop turned red. Once he recovered from the embarrassment of asking for directions to a place he was at, he proceeded to find a parking spot.

The gorge was exactly as Lena had described it. It sounded like one of those nature tapes my mom tried for relaxation. I wondered if this was where they recorded it. The water ran so quickly and was crystal clear. It wasn't deep, but rocks and boulders of all sizes dotted the stream. To our left were two fishermen.

"Catching anything?" T-Bone yelled.

"We are," one of the men answered with a smile, holding up a fish on his line.

"I guess you'll eat good tonight," said T-Bone.

"It's catch and release," the other man explained.

"I never tried that kind," T-Bone shrugged. "Is it good?"

"No," the man paused as he looked at the other fisherman. "These are fish that you *catch and release*."

"Then how do you eat them?" T-Bone wondered.

"You don't," the first man laughed. "We're fishing for sport."

"Hey, look," Timmy yelled. "Look at us."

We turned and saw Timmy and Wanda perched on rocks. This was exactly the type of activity my mom would have hated: crossing a stream of running water on slippery rocks. Since she wasn't here, we all gave it a try. One of the fishermen told us that in the summer, you'll find families with their chairs in the water watching their kids and dogs play in the cool stream. It sounded like a lot of fun.

"This is amazing!" Wanda yelled. "I love this place."

"I know," T-Bone agreed. "I bet most of the world doesn't even know about it."

"Most of the world?" I laughed. "I bet most of New Jersey doesn't even know about it."

We hopped from rock to rock while Pop and Timmy stood along the banks and took some pictures. Everyone made it to the other side without getting wet; well, almost everyone.

"Okay, Timmy," T-Bone instructed, "if you want to make it across the stream, it's more mental than physical. You need to think carefully. You want to plan each move; don't just jump. Think of crossing the stream like playing a game of chess. It's all about strategy and logic. Don't just hop around willy-nilly."

"Willy-nilly?" asked Timmy.

"Willy-nilly," T-Bone repeated. "It means haphazardly, just jumping around. You have to find rocks that are big enough. You have to find rocks that are dry. You have to find rocks that aren't covered with moss. You have to know exactly where you'll land. You have to picture your landing."

"That's a lot of stuff to think about," said Timmy.

"That's true," said T-Bone. "Maybe you'll understand my technique if I demonstrate exactly what you should do."

And with that, T-Bone began his trek across the stream. He started with a successful string of short, quick hops. He leaped from rock to rock like a gazelle. We all stood there in awe, amazed that he actually looked like he knew what he was doing. If professional rock hopper was a real thing, he totally could have been one. It was all going perfect until he landed on a particularly small rock. The landing was impressive; his feet barely fitting together. As he prepared for his next move, his right foot lifted up, and he landed in the stream. T-Bone stood there up to his knees in cold, running water. He was as shocked as we were. No one knew what went wrong. *No one except Timmy, that is.*

"Hey, T-Bone," he laughed. "There's one other thing you have to do."

"Really, Timmy?" asked a frustrated, cold, and wet T-Bone. "What could a beginner like you possibly tell a semi-pro like myself? Do you know anything about lift and drag? Do you know anything about velocity? How about air friction?"

"No," Timmy shook his head. "I don't know about that."

"Then what on earth could you possibly tell me?"

"Oh yeah," Timmy said as he pointed to T-Bone's feet, *"you have to tie your shoes!"*

"Don't worry, Tommy, I have a few towels," Pop said as he headed to the parking area. "Do me a favor and stay still until I come back."

I wasn't sure if T-Bone was mad at himself or simply embarrassed. His face was bright red, and his pants were soaked up to his knees. When he took a step, his saturated socks and sloshed sneakers squished and squeaked. He sounded like a puppy's chew toy. We all laughed about how he couldn't sneak up on anyone. Well, almost all of us laughed. *T-Bone definitely wasn't laughing.*

"Too soon?" I asked. The look he gave me confirmed that it was definitely too soon for him to laugh. I hoped this wouldn't turn into a Code Orange.

Luckily, the gorge was so awesome that T-Bone soon forgot all about his swan dive into the stream. The air was so clean that just breathing it made me feel healthier. There wasn't a cloud in the sky, and the sun poked through the canopy of trees overhead. I decided we definitely owed Lena Stein a big thank you when we posted our Kenneth Lockwood Gorge report.

As we continued to explore, we learned about the very memorable train wreck that occurred on Saturday, April 18, 1885. The central and southern spans of the 250-foot-long Ken Lockwood Gorge Bridge collapsed when a train loaded with iron ore started to cross. The forty-six-car train was coming from the iron mines to High Bridge. When the locomotive and first few cars passed over the bridge, the center and southern spans collapsed, dropping the locomotive to the hillside below. The rest of the train plunged sixty feet into the Raritan River. Daniel Bryant, the engineer, and John McGran, the locomotive fireman, jumped from the train, positive they were about to die. Fortunately, they both survived. Three other trainmen jumped to safety also. Henry Haltiman, the twenty-six-year-old head brakeman, wasn't as lucky. He was on top of the fifth freight car when the bridge collapsed. He desperately tried to apply the brakes, but it was too late, and he rode the freight car to his death.

"Wow," Wanda whispered. "I can't imagine how scary that must have been."

"I know," I agreed. "I probably would have been too scared to jump."

"Me, too," said Wanda. "I would have totally been paralyzed with fear."

"Not me," said a confident T-Bone. "I would have surveyed the situation, opened a window, and plotted my landing. There's plenty of time if you remain calm and don't panic."

"Hopefully, you would have had plenty of time to tie your shoe first," Timmy teased.

The whole time we explored the gorge, I wished I could tell the world that this amazing place was right here in New Jersey. I was tired of all of the negative things people said about the Garden State. I assumed most people who said negative things had never even been here. The others probably never left the airport while connecting to their next flight. They probably considered the industry and highways surrounding the Newark Liberty Airport as a sample of what the rest of the state looked like. It was too bad because New Jersey had so many different sides. The gorge was definitely a place people outside of New Jersey would never expect. I wished every New Jersey kid could visit it, too. Actually, I wished they could visit all of the places we had visited.

Luckily, T-Bone *kind of* asked his brother if he could borrow his GoPro camera again. And, luckily, his brother was sound asleep when he asked him. We couldn't fit every kid in the car with us, but we could share what we were seeing with the videos. I decided that was definitely the next best thing. It was a shame, however, that we missed T-Bone's swan dive.

As we left the gorge, we passed a house with a blue marker out front. Pop pulled up and we read it aloud: *Patriots imprisoned loyalist Pennsylvania Governor John Penn and Crown Supreme Court Justice Benjamin Chew here for several months during the Revolutionary War. They named the place SOLITUDE.*

It was a big, white house with porches and lots of windows. Wanda told us that the house was originally occupied by the superintendent of the Iron Works, and its famous guests included George and Martha Washington. Definitely not the worst pace for a loyalist to be imprisoned, I thought.

Our next stop was the Newark Museum and the Ballantine House. Wanda called David Dias to tell him we were heading that way. It was amazing how the western end of Interstate 78 was so mountainous and filled with towering trees and wide-open spaces. As we headed east, the terrain changed from mountains to cities. This, to me, was one of the best things about New Jersey. You could actually spend the day at a beach and the night at a mountain or in a city. In my opinion, our size and diversity made New Jersey the most amazing state.

As we entered the City of Newark, we could feel the excitement of a bustling city. The Newark Museum, on Washington Street, is the state's largest museum. It was established in 1909 in the Newark Public Library. Having David Dias offer to be our tour guide would really help us get the most out of our visit, and we were excited to get started. He was waiting inside the entrance with his dad, Luis, his mom, Fernanda, and his older brother, Samuel.

David was in fifth grade, but he seemed older. He was really smart and very mature. He told us he was in a gifted and talented program, and he really loved robotics. It only took T-Bone ten minutes to get his life story. It turned out he loved french fries, reading, writing, soccer, and swimming, but he wasn't a fan of heights. We immediately liked him. He was really nice and, like us, he loved New Jersey, too.

"So why do you love this museum so much?" asked Timmy.

"Well," David began. "It's educational and fun. I think you have to have both for kids to really learn."

"I agree," said Wanda. "People learn more and remember more if they have fun while they're learning."

"But I don't like art," said Timmy. "Do they have robots or dinosaurs?"

"I think a lot of kids come here thinking they don't like art and then leave here with a favorite type of art," David laughed. "They have so many kinds of art on display: American, Asian, African, classical, and even decorative."

"Uh-huh," Timmy nodded. "How about the robots?"

"Well," David continued, "they have creative play, where you can design take-home projects and even touch certain objects. The third floor has a Dynamic Earth exhibit and an exhibit called *emPowered* which is about renewable energy."

"In an art museum?" asked Timmy, suddenly perking up. "Can we start on the third floor?"

"Oh, and there's a planetarium," added David. "I saw an exhibit about the planet Saturn, which was once an ancient, wandering star."

"Can we go there, first?" Timmy asked, even more excited.

"How about we just follow David and enjoy the fact that we have a very knowledgeable guide," suggested Pop.

It was a good plan. We actually enjoyed the art. I loved the American art the most and even found a picture of Bordentown. As we made our way through the art galleries, David turned out to be a really great guide. If he wanted to, he would make an awesome teacher one day. I could see him leading his class on field trips or through math lessons. He told us when he grows up he wants to be the president, a surgeon, or an engineer. I figured he'd be great at anything.

We took the elevator to the third floor and were very excited when the doors opened. There were giant screens that said *Dynamic Earth: Revealing Nature's Secrets.* We watched a video and then came upon a hurricane machine. You stood inside and for one dollar, you could experience the force of Category 1 hurricane winds. It was awesome, and I couldn't imagine a Category 4 or 5. We explored the *emPowered* energy exhibits and learned about renewable energies like solar, wind, geothermal, and biomass. I never understood why, if fossil fuels were so bad for the environment and so many scientists found alternatives, we were still using fossil fuels. It didn't make sense. Hurting the earth if there is no other choice is bad enough, but hurting the earth when there are other ways to fuel things seemed kind of dumb. My dad always had the same answer: *if someone is getting rich, it won't change.* It was amazing how many things were controlled by money. It was kind of sad. I wondered where rich people would live when the earth was too damaged for humans.

Our next stop involved animal habitats, and my favorite was the polar bear perched upon an iceberg. It looked so real, and I wondered what the polar bears would sit on when the icebergs and glaciers were all gone.

The next exhibit that caught my eye was about New Jersey and Africa. While North America and North Africa are separated by four thousand miles, at one time, the continents were joined to form Pangaea, a supercontinent. When Pangaea split apart, the Atlantic Ocean was formed.

"Hey, Nick, look at that," said T-Bone, pointing to the exhibit. "These continents look like puzzle pieces that fit together."

"No kidding," I laughed. "This whole exhibit is showing you that the continents we know today were all connected. Look at this picture. That rock outcrop in Lyndhurst, New Jersey, is identical to the rock outcrop in Argana, Morocco, which is in North Africa."

"What are you trying to say?" asked T-Bone.

"I'm trying to say that at one point you could walk from Lyndhurst, New Jersey, to Argana, Morocco," I said.

"No way!" he exclaimed. "Are you serious?"

"Look," I replied as I pointed to a dial that allowed visitors to set the continents' movements in motion.

"South America fits in there, too," he yelled. "This is crazy."

"Why are you so shocked?" asked Wanda. "We learned about Pangaea in elementary school."

"Because this timeline shows them moving together and apart," T-Bone struggled to contain his excitement. "I didn't realize it was really real. I didn't know there was really a time when you could walk from North America to North Africa. Walt Disney really was right."

"Walt Disney was right about what?" I asked.

"It really is a small world after all!" T-Bone gushed.

We continued to follow David through the galleries and ended up at the Ballantine House. Even though it was currently connected to the museum, it was once the real home of the Ballantine family. It was huge and fancy, built in 1885 by John and Jeannette Ballantine on what was the very fashionable upper end of Washington Street. John's dad, Peter, a poor immigrant who came to America to start a new life, eventually started the Ballantine Brewery, living in a small house next door. Newark, in the 1840s, was beginning its rise as a major industrial center, leading in production of rubber, soap, beer, thread, glue, leather, and many other valuable commodities. That also meant the city was changing. The population in 1840, when Peter and Julia Ballantine brought their family to Newark, was 17,202. By 1870, the population was 105,059.

Clearly, the Ballantines were very wealthy. The first room we saw was the billiards room, complete with a pool table, fireplace, and a knight in shining armor. During that time, middle-class and upper-class people frowned upon visiting pool halls with working-class people.

"I would have done both," said T-Bone.

"You'd have frowned upon working-class people?" I asked.

"No, no, no," he shook his head. "I would have had a billiards room and visited the pool hall. I don't think people should judge other people by how much money they have."

Each room had lots of information about the room and the furnishings as well as notes. They really made it kid friendly. You didn't just walk through the home of a wealthy family. You understood how they lived, what they had, and what they didn't have compared to now.

The dining room was filled with a lot of objects, and etiquette was very important in the Victorian Era. It was the fanciest dining room I had ever seen. Even the ceiling was covered in gold. At first, I thought it must have been awesome to have been one of their guests. Then I changed my mind and realized I would have been too worried about doing something wrong to enjoy myself. Then I decided that if I had been invited, I could probably figure it all out. It didn't matter though, as the last dinner served by the Ballantines was a long, long time ago.

Even though this twenty-seven-room mansion was so massive, it still felt like a home. The decorations were warm and I was sure John and Jeannette's four kids must have loved it. At the top of the red-carpeted staircase was an enormous stained-glass-window. From the library to the bedrooms, it was so impressive. They even had games where you could guess the use of an object. With a music room, a library, a billiards room, a parlor, and a reception room, it felt like we were in the house from the board game *CLUE*.

"Did you know there's also a Fire Museum and a one-room schoolhouse?" asked David.

"No," we all said in unison.

"The Ballantines had their own firehouse?" asked Timmy.

"No, it's the Newark Fire Department's museum, and I think you'll like it," said David.

He was right. They had everything from the horse and stable days of firefighting to a modern-day fire engine. Well, the front of a fire engine, anyway; somehow, they must have cut a fire truck in half. There were display cases with real pictures, fire helmets, and even trumpets.

"Must have been a very musical department," said T-Bone. "Maybe it was a barbershop quartet but with firefighters."

"Actually," David explained, "those trumpets were used for communication before they had radios."

"Oh," said T-Bone.

"Hey, look," Timmy called from near the modern fire truck. He was standing in front of a locker wearing a turnout coat and a helmet. "Firefighter Timmy reporting for duty."

"Watch this," T-Bone said as he ran over and quickly put on a coat and helmet. "Captain T-Bone is on scene."

Wanda, David, and Samuel laughed as Timmy and T-Bone climbed into the front seat of the truck. A mural of a city street made the whole scene look very real. It only took a moment before T-Bone realized he was sitting behind the steering wheel, the place where the driver sits. Timmy was sitting in the front passenger seat, the place where the captain sits. Watching them try to switch seats while in the fire truck, without knocking off their helmets, was hysterical. It was like the public safety version of a clown car.

David pointed out the tools and also the real kitchen, where you must identify six fire hazards. I thought it was a great way to teach kids about safety because they made it fun. He showed us a sign that explained the history of the building. It was once the carriage house of Marcus L. Hook, a member of Hook and Ladder Co. No. 1. He also served as governor of New Jersey from 1865-1868.

"Could you imagine burning your dinner, and the governor shows up to put out the fire?" asked T-Bone.

"No," Pop shook his head. "I can't."

We saw a fire pole, the furnace, the safe where they kept the firemen's pension records, and the ticker tape that was used to report emergencies long before 9-1-1.

"You know," said David, "the first fire alarms were church bells."

"No way!" I exclaimed, trying to imagine church bells relaying such important information.

"Then in 1870, when Newark had over one-hundred-thousand people, the first alarm telegraph system was installed. It electrically connected forty miles of overhead wire, sixty street boxes, and three church bells."

"How the heck…" T-Bone began to ask.

"Well," David continued, "when a street corner alarm box was activated, an alarm went to the central office, and they sent telegraphs to all of the firehouses with the location."

"That's amazing," I said. It was always so interesting to see the baby steps technology has taken. I wondered what my grandkids would think about our high-tech devices and gadgets. I wondered if they would think we had it rough, just like every generation always feels about previous generations.

"David, can we see the schoolhouse?" asked Wanda.

"Absolutely," he smiled.

He led us through the Alice Ransom Dreyfuss Memorial Garden and toward the 1784 Old Stone Schoolhouse, the oldest standing building in Newark. George Washington even visited the school on his way to the Battle of Elizabeth.

"This isn't the original site," said David. "It used to be on Pot Pie Lane, a small road connecting Newark and Elizabethtown, and it was called the Chancellor School. In 1938, the Newark Board of Education gave it to the Newark Museum, and it was moved, stone by stone, to the gardens."

"I don't know what's better," T-Bone shrugged, "a street named for pot pies or moving a school one stone at a time."

The Chancellor School that sits on the original site was built in 1938 and is still operating. In 2007, the staff and students opened up a time capsule from 1938 and replaced the contents with modern items. It was such a great story. The plaque outside was very old and had turned green, but we were able to read the inscription:

Two Centuries Ago, on this spot, the seed of Newark's educational system was planted. The Parent School, built in 1728 and burned in 1782 was succeeded by this structure in 1784. Within these modest walls many of New Jersey's leaders received their early training. Before this door, in 1797, George Washington paused to acknowledge the homage of the pupils. Its early mission completed, this schoolhouse stands a memorial of our forefathers' far-visioned creed that government by the people must be founded on education of the people. It was dedicated November 3, 1924.

"See," T-Bone said, pointing at the plaque.

"See what?" I asked, looking through the windows at the desks, blackboard, pot-belly stove, and supplies.

"See what it says! Even our forefathers knew that a good government requires the education of the people," he replied. "That's what I've been saying."

"I agree," said Wanda, much to T-Bone's delight. "Everyone should have access to a quality, free public education."

"What if you want to go to a fancy school?" asked Timmy.

"There's nothing wrong with attending a, as you call it, fancy school," said Pop. "In America, we have that choice. But those decisions should never hurt the public schools."

"What if a public school isn't doing well?" I asked.

"That's a different issue," said Pop. "If a public school isn't succeeding, it's not because it's a *public school*. Generally speaking, it's usually linked to poverty and/or much bigger issues."

"David, where do you go to school?" asked Timmy.

"I go to Hamilton School in Harrison," he said.

"Is it real far?" I asked.

"No, it's about a mile away," he replied.

"You're lucky," said Timmy. "I would hang out here all of the time if I lived a mile away."

"That's the great thing about New Jersey, though," I said. "Even if you live at the farthest points of the state, you're still not that far from other places in New Jersey."

"True," said Pop. "Very, very true. The key is making sure people know how amazing this state is, which is what you kids have been doing."

We completed our tour and walked back to the museum entrance. David's parents were waiting for him and Samuel. We were sad to say goodbye. He was really smart and so much fun to hang out with. We thanked him for the tour and for sharing the City of Newark with us. His idea to visit the museum was brilliant. Even Timmy, who was less than excited to visit an art museum, had a great time. It just goes to show you that you never know whether you'll really like something until you try it. Luckily, we were all pretty adventurous and open to trying new things.

Like Trenton, Newark had so much energy. We passed some parks with enormous statues, and I noticed a large statue of Christopher Columbus. I remembered Trenton had one right in Columbus Park. Pop told us that the Passaic River was to Newark as the Delaware River was to Trenton. Even though Newark was bigger, both cities were so important to New Jersey's past, present, and future. I hoped Newark had a coalition of dedicated people like the Capital City Community Coalition. Like Mayor Jackson said, you should never underesimate the power of dedicated people with good ideas.

On our ride home, T-Bone sat in the back seat right between Timmy and Wanda. I was pretty sure he was praying Wanda would fall asleep on his shoulder. A few minutes later, I realized someone did fall asleep on his shoulder; *unfortunately, it was Timmy.*

CHAPTER ELEVEN

The day after our gorge/museum trip, I was exhausted. Wanda offered to write the reports, and I couldn't have been happier. When I woke up, I looked over her plan for CODE READ. It was great, but it would definitely be a lot of work. Luckily, she included the numbers of the fire department union officials who would be able to help us. She gave me the phone numbers for Firefighter Wayne Wolk and Chief Steve Coltre. I learned that they were the presidents of the FMBA Locals 6 and 206. I didn't know what that meant. They explained that it stood for the Fireman's Mutual Benevolent Association, which was the firefighters' union. The union supported many programs for city residents, and they both offered their services to help us coordinate everything. Boy, they help everyone in need, I thought.

Within two weeks, we had already collected thousands of books. As I watched the piles of books grow, I was shocked. It was so much more successful than I ever imagined. While most people saw a training room filled with books, I saw something else. I saw kids holding their own book and smiling. I wanted every kid in Trenton to have at least one book to call their own.

My mom brought us to fire headquarters night after night so we could organize the piles. Wanda contacted Wilfredo Ortiz at the Board of Education, his assistant Marizol Tirado, and a woman named Tonya Grant to figure out how many kids were in each school and in each class. We wanted to give each teacher a bag of books that matched the ages of each student. Just when I thought we would never get all of the bags filled, nine college kids wearing blue shirts, black pants, and black boots walked through the door. They were the college students from FEMA Corps. They told us that they commit to volunteering to help where help is needed, and at the end of their time, they receive some money for college. Their program sounded like an amazing way to help those in need, see the country, and learn the real meaning of teamwork. It was a massive operation, and I was sure we had collected enough books. Unfortunately, even with the towering piles we still needed two thousand more to reach all pre-K through fifth-grade students in the public schools.

"Nick, if we can come up with two thousand more books, we can make sure every school gets books," said T-Bone.

"That's what I'm worried about," I admitted. "What if we don't get them? How do we decide which schools get books and which schools don't get books?"

"Think positive," he said. "And if we don't get them all by this weekend, ask Wanda what to do. She knows what to do about everything."

He was kind of right. Wanda probably would know. On the bright side, we had already collected almost five thousand books. We were in the home stretch. While T-Bone and I tried to think about ways to get those extra books, Wanda had already beat us to a solution.

"So according to my calculations, for CODE READ to cover every public elementary school in the city, we need twenty-two-hundred more books," she announced.

"Great," I mumbled. "That's two hundred more than what I thought we needed."

"It is great," she continued. "I spoke with the New Jersey Education Association, and they are sending over several hundred books. Thomas Edison State College and Saint Paul's church are sending over boxes and boxes of books. And we're going to take the money donated by the unions to buy books at the Hamilton Township library."

"Question," said T-Bone. "How do you buy books at a library? Isn't that where you borrow books? Isn't that why you have a library card?"

"Actually," Wanda explained, "the Friends of the Library organization holds book sales several times a year."

"Question," said T-Bone. "How can we afford to buy 1,500 books? We didn't get that many donations, did we?"

"The books at the book sale usually cost between ten cents and a dollar," she said. "I spoke to Betty and Mary Linda, and they said they should have enough picture books, easy readers, chapter books, and novels. They were very helpful."

"You really did your homework, huh?" I asked.

"Don't I always?" she said smugly, but with a smile.

The last few days of CODE READ were a blur. The weather was changing, and days were getting shorter. The only thing that seemed to be getting longer was my list of homework assignments. We arrived at the Friends of the Library, and off-duty firefighters met us there with pickup trucks. Captain Dave Smolka and Firefighters Bobby Bland and Akyise Watkins led the group as they helped us pick out the books and load them in their trucks. When we got back to headquarters, Wanda did a final tally of the books.

"Okay," she sighed. "Four hundred short. Any ideas?"

"Actually, yes," said T-Bone. "I think we should stop by Barnes & Noble and ask if they have any books to donate."

"That could work," agreed Wanda. "But let's call first."

While T-Bone called Barnes & Noble, I remembered where

I could get several boxes, and I quickly called George. He wasn't just happy to donate the books; he offered to deliver them and lend a hand. That evening, George and two of his neighbors arrived with several boxes.

"Did someone order some kids' books?" he asked as they filed into the room, boxes in tow.

"Hey, George," said T-Bone. "You could have called us if you needed some work done."

"Actually, we're donating books," he explained.

"Oh, that's a relief!" said T-Bone. "Because we're pretty swamped."

"I see that," he nodded.

"How did you make out with Barnes & Noble?" I asked.

"Oh, right," said T-Bone. "I spoke with the Community Relations Director, Susan Hogan, and she had some titles she could give us. I still cannot believe how generous everyone is."

"Things like this really bring out the best in people. How about we give you a ride to pick them up?" asked George.

"Sounds good," I agreed.

Wanda decided to stay behind, sorting and counting, while we picked up the books. There were so many people contributing, and in two days we would be delivering the books to the schools. When we arrived at Barnes & Noble, we asked for Susan. She met us by the café and told us that she admired our work. She asked us if we minded waiting a few minutes, and she headed to the back of the store.

While we waited, T-Bone started talking to a kid who was waiting for his mom to come back from the café. In typical T-Bone fashion, he knew his life story in three minutes.

"Nick, come meet my new friend, Nick," he said. "Get it? His name is Nick, too."

"Yeah, I get it," I nodded. "Hi, Nick, how are you?"

"Good," he said. "How are you?"

"So I told Nick about what we were doing, and he thought it was a great idea," said T-Bone. "He's actually a YES! Ambassador. They're Youth Examples of Self-Advocacy."

"That's great," I said. "What's a YES! Ambassador?"

Nick explained that he had dyslexia, and he volunteers for Learning Ally to share tips and new technology with younger kids who have dyslexia. I thought it was brilliant. No one can help a kid with dyslexia more than someone who has gone through it, too.

"What's it like?" asked T-Bone.

"Are you crazy?" I asked him as I slapped his shoulder. "I don't think you should ask that."

"It's okay," he nodded. "It's kind of difficult before you're diagnosed. That's when you're struggling, and no one knows why. That's the toughest part."

"Do you use sign language?" asked T-Bone. "Read lips?"

"He's not deaf," I said.

"Oh, that's right," said T-Bone. "Do you use Braille? Or books on tape?"

"He's not blind either," I corrected him again. Some days, I wished he had an off button.

"Okay, does dyslexia mean your throat swells up when you eat a peanut or get stung by a bee?"

"Not even close," Nick laughed. "Those are allergies."

"Okay, I give up," said T-Bone. "What is dyslexia?"

"It's a learning difference that usually affects reading, writing, and spelling because it's difficult to associate sounds and letters," he explained. "It's not uncommon. Lots of very famous and successful people have had dyslexia."

"Oh, I get it," said T-Bone. "Now are you an Official Ambassador?"

"Yup," he said. "It's pretty cool."

"What makes someone dyslexic?" T-Bone continued.

"Well, if you have dyslexia, you process information in a different part of the brain," he explained.

"So it's like a real estate problem?" T-Bone guessed.

"Huh?" Nick and I said at the same time.

"You know, location, location, location," said T-Bone.

"Do a lot of people have it?" I asked, ignoring T-Bone.

"It's actually about one in five people, but it often goes undiagnosed," he said. "That's a very big problem."

"I can imagine," I said, wondering how many people fail to succeed in school because of an undiagnosed learning disability. "How do you help others as a YES! Ambassador?"

"As a YES! Ambassador, I tell other kids about the latest technology like audiobooks and things like special tutoring. It's also good, no matter what challenge you face, to talk to people who've faced the same issue. I think that's one of the best things we do; showing people how we deal with it."

By the time Susan returned with our donation, we had made a new friend and learned about something we never really understood. If we could teach people about education, poverty, and the importance of books for kids as easily as Nick explained dyslexia, we really could spark lasting changes in the world.

After we met his mom, Denise, and his sister, Natalie, we thanked Nick and told him to keep up the good work. On the way back, we told George all about our conversation.

"I know all about dyslexia," he said with a smile.

"How do you know?" asked T-Bone.

"My nephew is dyslexic," he replied.

"That's a shame," said T-Bone.

"Not really," George laughed. "He's an engineer and probably one of the smartest people I know."

"Really?" I asked.

"Absolutely," he nodded. "My sister always told him that it's not a game-ender; it's simply a game-changer. He just changed the way he learned. From what I know, those with dyslexia have either average or above-average intelligence. And they're often very creative."

It was amazing to me that years ago, someone with dyslexia could be considered a poor student when they just needed a new way to learn. By spreading awareness and helping those who have been diagnosed, Nick and the other ambassadors were doing something amazing.

As we pulled into fire headquarters and entered the training room, we placed three boxes on the table. Wanda carefully opened each box, counted all of the books, and smiled.

"Can I have everyone's attention?" she announced as the room became silent. "With the donations we just received, we are now thirty-one books over our goal!"

Everyone started cheering and high-fiving each other. There was such a feeling of relief and accomplishment. Every-where you looked, the whole room was filled with smiles. We stayed extra late that night, filling the bags and attaching Nicky Fifth CODE READ labels.

On the two mornings we planned to deliver the books, we arrived at the firehouse at 7:00 am. My family came, along with Pop, T-Bone, Wanda, and George. There were off-duty firefighters with their kids, and volunteers from the coalition. We loaded the bags and proceeded to our first school. With Firefighter Nasib driving the chief's car to lead the caravan and with Captain Todd's crew from Engine 3 at the end of a line of pickup trucks, we worked our way through the city. On the first day, we visited eight schools, providing every teacher with a bag containing enough books for every student. The students had no idea we were coming, and their excitement was all of the thanks anyone needed. They were hugging their new books and thanking everyone. Some asked for the firefighters' autographs, and others told us they couldn't wait to go home and read their new book.

"It's a beautiful thing you kids have done," my mom whispered as a boy picked T-Bone up and twirled him around. "Look, Nick, this is pure happiness."

By lunchtime, we were on our way back to school and excited to continue the next day. Our teachers didn't mind our absence and seemed really proud of CODE READ. Our principal, who donated books, even welcomed us back with an announcement telling the school what we had done.

The next morning, even more volunteers showed up. When we arrived at the fourth school, we noticed a familiar face.

"Nick, look at that guy over there," he said, pointing to a tall gentleman in a dark suit. "That's the guy with the easy license plate number."

"No, T-Bone," I laughed, "I think that's Mayor Jackson."

"Good morning, boys," he said as he walked over and shook our hands. "This is a wonderful thing you've done."

"Thank you, your highness," said T-Bone as he bowed and curtsied at the same time.

"Sounds like you just promoted me to royalty," he smiled.

"We didn't promote you, but we did join the coalition like you suggested," said T-Bone. "They're helping us with our goals; mine is education, Wanda's is poverty, and Nick is focused on giving kids books to keep."

"From where I stand," the Mayor said, "you've hit all three. You're giving books to kids, which is your goal, Nicky. By giving to kids who may not own many books, you're addressing poverty, Wanda. And by getting kids excited about reading, you're addressing education, T-Bone."

"I didn't look at it that way," I nodded, feeling even prouder.

"Remember, books, poverty, and education all directly impact kids," he explained. "So on behalf of the City of Trenton, I thank you and hope you'll continue to work here."

"You wouldn't have the power to appoint us Official Junior Ambassadors, would you?" T-Bone inquired.

"No," he smiled, "but if you need a reference, just holler."

I couldn't believe we did it. I never felt prouder. The kids we met were funny, smart, and really friendly, the same as the kids we meet everywhere. Poverty didn't affect who they were. CODE READ really showed the power of people coming together. At the end, I couldn't figure out who felt better, the kids or the volunteers. *It was definitely a tie.*

CHAPTER TWELVE

The next morning, T-Bone boarded the school bus with his usual smile.

"Nick, Nick," he said. "Do you believe we did it? Do you believe we gave out over seven thousand books?"

I couldn't believe it myself. I tried to concentrate on my schoolwork, but my mind was racing again. By the time lunch rolled around, all I wanted to do was plan more events. Wanda joined us for a while and told us she received a call from Tonya Grant at the Trenton Board of Education.

"She said her brother, Greg, has a foundation called 94 Feet," Wanda explained.

"He must need a lot of shoes," laughed T-Bone.

"Really?" Wanda glared at him. "It's actually called *94 Feet* because that's the length of a basketball court."

"I don't get it," I said.

"Greg is Trenton-born and raised, and he attended Trenton State College before the name changed to The College of New Jersey," she continued. "Then he played in the NBA."

"No way!" I exclaimed. "What team? How many years? Is he like nine feet tall?"

"Well, he holds so many records at Trenton State College, and he holds the national record for points scored in one season with 1,044," she began. "He's the all-time lead-scoring player for all of New Jersey. He was drafted by Phoenix but also played for New York, Philadelphia, and Denver. And he's not nine feet tall. He's actually 5'7" tall."

"That's not big in the NBA," I said. "He must be a hustler."

"He is. He started the foundation to help kids through sports, and now the focus is on academics. He runs after-school programs and camps at the Trenton Pubic Schools."

"Are you serious?" I asked. "That's amazing."

"So Tonya thought we might be able to work with Greg on some of his projects," she said.

"I'm in!" exclaimed T-Bone. "I am so in. Unless you have to actually play basketball; then I'm out. I'm kind of a klutz on a basketball court. Or a baseball field. Or a hockey rink."

"I don't think a former NBA player needs you to play," she laughed.

"Then I'm definitely in," said T-Bone.

"Me, too," I agreed.

"Great; I'll set up a meeting."

A few days later, we went to Martin Luther King School to meet with Greg Grant at his after-school program. Wanda told him how much his sister, Tonya, helped with CODE READ, and he smiled proudly.

"I saw you in the *Times of Trenton*," he said. "Kevin Shea wrote a fantastic article about your efforts. Great job!"

"What?" T-Bone jumped up. "We're in the paper?"

"Oh, I thought you saw it," he laughed. "Here, you can take this one and make some copies and it's also on nj.com."

"Thanks," I said, trying to contain my excitement.

"So I thought you kids might want to get involved with my foundation," he suggested. "I haven't thought it all through yet, but I like what you're doing."

While he spoke to us, little kids were coming up and handing him envelopes or just saying hello. Even though he was speaking to us, he managed to smile at every kid who came by. He told us that he started the foundation when he was twenty-seven years old, after he retired from basketball. Soon, the conversation drifted to kids in need.

"The thing many folks forget," he said, "is that kids who live in poverty don't have the same resources as other kids. From books to food and, for some kids, even a place to live. They don't have the same experiences. Some of these kids are even afraid to walk to school."

"That's terrible," said T-Bone. "They should take a bus."

"This is a walking district," said Greg. "If a child lives within two miles of their school, there's no bus."

"So you mean, if a kid lives 1.9 miles away, they have to walk to school?" asked T-Bone. "That's an outrage. Plus, that's a lot of streets to cross. And what about bad weather?"

"Still walking," said Greg. "In the winter, you see moms pushing strollers through ice and snow to get their older kids to school. Like I said, it's a different experience because they have different resources."

"That's what Wanda is focused on," I said, pointing to her. "She wants to destroy poverty. And she means it."

"That's great," he said, "because poverty's a big issue. It will take a lot of determined, great minds to conquer it."

"Can I ask you a question?" I said.

"Sure," he replied. "What's on your mind?"

"Haven't people been trying to conquer poverty for a really long time?" I asked. "Why hasn't it worked yet?"

"You really know how to ask a question," he laughed, clearly expecting a much simpler question.

"Well, I mean, if kids want to help," I began, "how do we avoid doing all of the things that don't work?"

"That's a good question," he nodded. "And you're right; many of the things we do to address poverty aren't done because they work, but because that's what we've always done. I think the biggest problem is that people don't understand what poverty really is, and that's what makes it hard to solve."

"My mom says that to change the way people act, we have to change the way people see things," I said.

"Like with education," T-Bone chimed in, "many schools that aren't doing well also have high poverty. And it's not just in the cities; it's in rural areas, too."

"But the solutions never address the actual poverty," said Wanda. "Creating more curriculums, more standardized tests, and more paperwork doesn't make any sense."

"You've really given this a lot of thought," he nodded. "And, I agree, we cannot expect the same results from kids with every resource as we do from kids with limited resources."

"My mom is a teacher," I said, "and she tells us about kids who start kindergarten without knowing an *A* from a *G* while other kids start kindergarten reading whole books."

"Sadly," he agreed, "that gap only gets wider as the kids get older. So what does that tell you?"

"Oh, I get it," said Wanda.

"You do?" asked T-Bone.

"Sure, like Nick's grandfather says, we need to concentrate on kids before they reach school, during the first five years," she replied. "And we need to help young families start off on the right foot to give people hope."

"That's kind of mean to the kids who are already in school," T-Bone pointed out. "Are you gonna just leave them out?"

"I never said to forget them," Wanda defended herself. "I think they need different resources, like enrichment, summer school, smaller classes, more teachers' aides, and alternatives, like vocational skills and the arts."

"I agree," said Greg. "If we implement the things that will actually make a difference, we'll start to see results. Just like playing ball, it takes a team. A college degree isn't the only goal. The job or career that allows people to earn a living should be the goal. College, a trade, or job skills all do that."

He told us about a gentleman named Juan Martinez who created a backpack drive and family events for the kids in the Trenton Public Schools. He worked tirelessly to get donations of backpacks and supplies. He had even created parent workshops. Very smart, I thought.

"We need more people like Juan," said T-Bone.

"We can help him," I suggested.

"Unfortunately, he passed away," said Greg, "but his legacy continues, and we'll continue to give back in his name."

While we were sad to hear that someone as committed to Trenton's kids as Juan had passed away, we were glad we learned about his work. We also learned that Greg worked closely with the Bonner Foundation to provide much-needed programs and resources. He told Wanda she should learn more about their work to support antipoverty programs in the area of education and hunger. I knew she would know everything about them by the next morning, *if not sooner.*

Our meeting with Greg inspired us. He faced billion-to-one odds to get drafted in the NBA as a 5'7" player, yet he did it. And when he retired, he decided to give back. When I told my dad who we met, he looked very impressed.

"Why are you so impressed?" I asked. "Is it because of his records or that he played for four NBA teams?"

"That's definitely impressive," my dad agreed. "But I've read about him, and I think it's his work off the court that's even more impressive."

"How do you know about Greg?" I asked.

"I've read stories here and there over the years. *He's really a hometown hero.*"

While Timmy and my dad watched a movie and my mom gave my sisters a bath, I called T-Bone. His mom said he was on his way to my house. I should have known. I decided to sit on the front porch and wait. A few minutes later, T-Bone was standing in front of my house.

"Going somewhere?" I said from the darkness, hoping for once I would startle him like he always startles me.

"Going here," he calmly answered, as if he was expecting me to be sitting there.

"Of course you are," I laughed. "What's up?"

"I heard this song today, and it made me think about what we're trying to do," he said. "It was on my mom's playlist."

"It's not a love song for Wanda, I hope."

"No, but that's a good idea," he nodded. "Maybe I should find *our* song."

"I know a song that would work," I played along. "I think it's called *Hit the Road Jack and Don't You Come Back No More.*"

"That won't work," he said, after giving it some thought. "My name's not even Jack."

"So what's this great song?" I asked.

"It's called *Waiting on the World to Change* by John Mayer," he explained. "It's all about how hard it is for new generations to change things. I think it should be our theme song."

"Our theme song?" I laughed. "We're not starring in a movie. Why do we need a theme song?"

"All great movements have a theme song," he said. "Here, listen."

T-Bone pulled out an iPod and played the song. I had to admit it: if we were starring in a movie, it would be a great theme song. It was brilliant. My favorite part was about seeing what's wrong but feeling like we don't have the tools necessary to change things.

T-Bone was right; it was really good. We listened to it so much that the next morning, I woke up humming it. It was like John Mayer understood what we were trying to do. It

...so explained why so many people don't get involved. Most people think they can't do anything, so they're just waiting for the world to change. I wanted to tell every kid to download it and really listen to the words. It was that good.

At lunch the next day, T-Bone called Wanda to our table. I assumed he was going to *tell* her all about the song. Instead, he started singing it loudly. He sang every single word. By the time he got to the second verse, a small crowd had gathered. With each verse, Wanda grew a little redder, and the crowd grew a little bigger. And T-Bone, he just kept singing louder.

When he sang the last word, he stood there smiling, waiting for applause. It was the most awkward, silent moment of my life. I didn't know what to do, so I started clapping. Just when I thought T-Bone couldn't possibly recover from the embarassment, something strange happened. Wanda started to clap, too. While the two of us clapped, I waited for everyone else to join in. It felt like T-Bone was starring in one of those movies where the crowd lifts the main character onto their shoulders and parades him around, cheering all the while.

Unfortunately, T-Bone was starring in a different movie. In this movie, two people clapped, and everyone else stared. The funny thing was, T-Bone didn't even care that he had embarassed himself in front of a cafeteria full of middle-school kids. It didn't matter. The only thing he saw was his two best friends clapping.

As the crowd dispersed, T-Bone sat back down. I was still in shock and wasn't sure what to say next. Thankfully, Wanda always knew what to do and say. She sat down next to him and told him she thought it was a perfect theme song. I still didn't know why three kids trying to change the world needed a soundtrack, but if we were going to have one, this was a really good song. Wanda then told him about a song called *Where is the Love?* by the Black Eyed Peas. She said it was one of those remakes where they changed the words. She told us that it really captured everything that was wrong in the world. I was so confused. I really needed to start listening to more music. The only songs I could even think of were Christmas carols, *Happy Birthday*, and Louis Armstrong's *What a Wonderful World,* and that was only because it was my kindergarten graduation song, and we sang it all year to get ready.

While they compared lyrics, *What a Wonderful World* started playing in my head. This time, I actually found myself listening to the words. Maybe, if we tried hard enough, we would help make the world a little more wonderful for everyone.

That night, before I went to bed, T-Bone called me.

"Nick, I have one of those good news, bad news things," he said. "I'll give you the bad news first. Wanda has stopped using her strawberry shampoo."

"Thanks for the heads-up," I sighed. "I'll alert the media."

"Before you get upset," he continued, "there's good news."

"Okay, what's the good news?"

"It's really good," he gushed. "It's about her new shampoo."

"Let me guess," I played along. "Banana? Pear? Taco salad? Rocky Road? Peanut butter? Asparagus? Pine tree?"

"No, no, no," he interupted. "Except for the pear, they're really all ridiculous guesses. Seriously? Banana? You better keep guessing."

"You do realize you're talking to a guy that doesn't even know what scent his own shampoo is, right?" I said.

"Okay, then, since you're begging me, I'll just tell you," he announced. "It's still so hard to believe, but I recognized it as soon as she sat down today, Wanda's new shampoo... *mango-coconut-papaya!*"

The End

Nicky Fifth's New Jersey Contest

Are You a New Jersey Character?

Lisa Funari-Willever is always looking for great ideas and places for Nicky, T-Bone, and Wanda to explore. Over the years, many of her best ideas have come from students and teachers she meets during her School Author Visits.

Submit your favorite New Jersey destination to Nicky Fifth, T-Bone, and Wanda, and you could become a character in an upcoming Nicky Fifth book. Write a 3-4 paragraph persuasive essay, selling your idea. Make sure your idea is located in New Jersey and hasn't been included in a previous book in the series. Check the website for a list of places already included.

Entries are judged on creativity, writing style, history, and level of persuasion. Do not list numerous locations; focus on one, and make sure it is located in New Jersey. To enter, visit www.nickyfifth.com, and be sure you have your parents' permission.

Prizes:

1st Prize
$200.00 Barnes & Noble Gift Card
***YOUR* idea is used in an upcoming book**
***YOU* become a character in the book**

2nd Prize
$100.00 Barnes & Noble Gift Card

3rd Prize
$75.00 Barnes & Noble Gift Card

Tips:

1. Only select New Jersey locations.

2. Do not write more than 3-4 persuasive paragraphs. If you write more or less, you will be disqualified.

3. Be creative and remember that the characters love history when selecting your location.

4. Include all of your contact information and make sure you use your phone number, not your school's phone number.

Nicky Fifth's New Jersey
Contest Winners

1st Place - David Dias
Hamilton School, Harrison, NJ
Newark Museum

2nd Place - Lena Stein
Old Farmers Road School, Long Valley, NJ
Kenneth Lockwood Gorge

3rd Place - Tie - Adam Bandler
Marlboro Elementary School, Marlboro, NJ
Trenton, New Jersey

3rd Place - Tie - Shreya Bhardwaj
Irwin Elementary School, East Brunswick, NJ
Princeton, New Jersey

NFF

Nicky Fifth Foundation

About the Nicky Fifth Foundation

In May 2015, after years of providing tens of thousands of free books to schools and children in need, Lisa Funari-Willever created the Nicky Fifth Foundation to promote literature, education, and awareness for New Jersey children.

With the help of her husband, Todd Willever, and good friend, Iris Hutchinson, the foundation was born. The first step was establishing a dynamic Board of Directors to guide the foundation. Luckily, Lisa knew many dynamic people.

One by one, the board seats were entusiastically occupied by individuals who really care about New Jersey kids. Along with Lisa, Todd, and Iris, the Board of Directors consists of Paula Agabiti, Karen Funari, Dawn Hiltner, Don Jay Smith, Walker Worthy, Brenda Zanoni, and Nancy Byrne.

Once the board was established, the first program, Nicky Fifth's CODE READ, began.

CODE RE*A*D

by the Nicky Fifth Foundation

As you read the story and came upon Nicky Fifth's CODE READ, you may have assumed it was pure fiction; a good idea, but pure fiction. Well, it was a great idea, and it really happened. The Nicky Fifth Foundation worked closely with the Trenton Fire Department and their unions, FMBA Locals 6 and 206, the New Jersey Education Association, FEMA Corps, the Mercer County Prosecutors Office, churches, and numerous individuals and volunteers to collect over seven thousand children's books.

Working out of Trenton Fire Headquarters, books were sorted and bagged. A bag was prepared for every Pre-K through 5th grade teacher in all fifteen Trenton Public Schools. This massive operation was completed in five weeks. Starting on June 23, 2015, CODE READ spent two days delivering books to every public school in the city.

As a caravan of on/off-duty firefighters and volunteers, led by fire vehicles, wound through the city, children saw their heroes responding to a very different type of crisis. With four out of five city libraries closed for over five years, CODE READ saved the day.

But providing books to keep was just the very first step: Phase 1. Three weeks later, the firefighters worked with the Nicky Fifth Foundation to implement Phase 2 and place books in three Trenton firehouses. City children can now check out the firehouses while they check out a book. Through the Trenton Firefighters' Book Club, children receive a library card, borrow books, and get to know the heroes in their neighborhood.

Phase 3 places firefighters in the schools, on a regular basis, to read with students. This not only shows students how important reading is, it creates a greater sense of community.

As the first CODE READ city, Trenton has welcomed the program and thoroughly supports the foundation's work. But, this is just the beginning. The Nicky Fifth Foundation plans to expand to other cities in need across the Garden State. We invite students, teachers, and families to join our effort and ensure every New Jersey child has books at home and easy access to borrowing books.

If you or your school would like to join Nicky Fifth's CODE READ or our other vital programs, visit www.nickyfifth.org. Get informed, get involved, and change lives!

Passport to the Garden State

How to Use the Passport

Unlike some of our previous passport books, this one is a bit different. Because some of the destinations are natural or historic landmarks, having a person available to stamp your book is not always possible.

To make it easier for families to complete the passport, this passport does not require you to locate a stamp. For this passport, simply use the white boxes to fill in the date you have visited each destination.

Visit as many, if not all, of the amazing destinations from this book to see firsthand what makes New Jersey so amazing.

Visit the nickyfifth.com website for a link to check hours, fees, menus, etc., and then have your own *Garden State Adventure!*

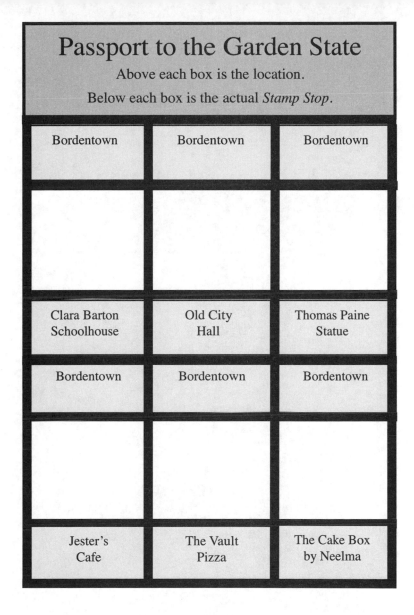

Passport to the Garden State

Above each box is the location.

Below each box is the actual *Stamp Stop*.

Bordentown	Bordentown	Bordentown
Clara Barton Schoolhouse	Old City Hall	Thomas Paine Statue
Bordentown	Bordentown	Bordentown
Jester's Cafe	The Vault Pizza	The Cake Box by Neelma

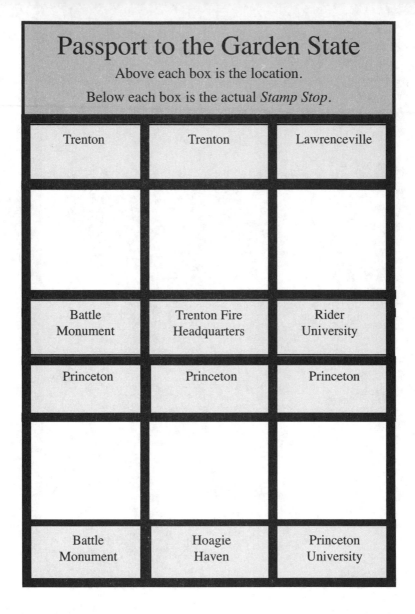

Passport to the Garden State

Above each box is the location.

Below each box is the actual *Stamp Stop*.

Trenton	Trenton	Lawrenceville
Battle Monument	Trenton Fire Headquarters	Rider University
Princeton	Princeton	Princeton
Battle Monument	Hoagie Haven	Princeton University

Passport to the Garden State

Above each box is the location.

Below each box is the actual *Stamp Stop*.

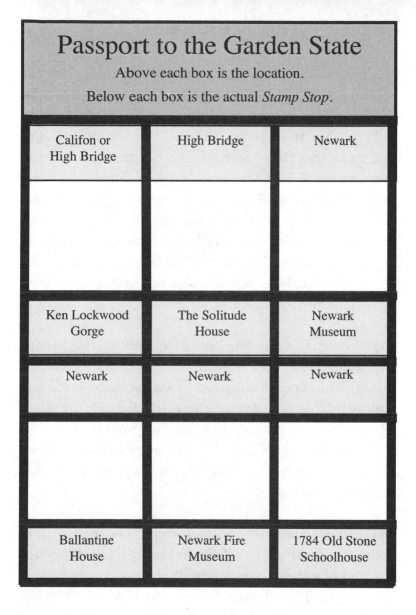

Califon or High Bridge	High Bridge	Newark
Ken Lockwood Gorge	The Solitude House	Newark Museum
Newark	Newark	Newark
Ballantine House	Newark Fire Museum	1784 Old Stone Schoolhouse

About the Author

Lisa Funari-Willever wanted to be an author since she was in the third grade. She has been a wedding dress seller, a file clerk, a sock counter (*really*), a hostess, waitress, teacher, and author. While she loved teaching in Trenton, New Jersey, becoming an author has been one of the most exciting adventures of her life. She is a full-time mom and a nighttime author who travels all over the world visiting schools. She has been to hundreds of schools in dozens of states, including California, South Dakota, Iowa, South Carolina, Florida, Delaware, Connecticut, New York, Pennsylvania, Ohio, Nevada, Idaho, Utah, Alabama, Louisiana, and even the U.S. Navy base in Sasebo, Japan.

She has written twenty-four books for children and teachers. *A Glove of Their Own* won the 2009 Benjamin Franklin Award. The critically acclaimed *Chumpkin* was selected as a favorite by First Lady Laura Bush and displayed at the White House; *Everybody Moos at Cows* was featured on the *Rosie O'Donnell Show*; and *Garden State Adventure* and *32 Dandelion Court* have been frequent selections on the New Jersey Battle of the Books list.

Lisa, a graduate of Trenton State College, is married to Todd Willever, a captain in the Trenton Fire Department. They reside in Mansfield, New Jersey (Burlington County), with their three children, Jessica, Patrick, and Timothy. If you'd like Lisa to come to your school for an Author Visit, go to www.franklinmasonpress.com for details.